It happened in
Ghana

A Historical Romance 1824-1971

Noel Smith

 SUB-SAHARAN PUBLISHERS

This edition published in 2007 by
SUB-SAHARAN PUBLISHERS
P.O. BOX LG358,
LEGON, ACCRA, GHANA

Originally published in 2005 in Germany by
Noel Smith Publications.

ISBN: 978-9988-647-26-1

Typesetting and Cover design by Kwabena Agyepong

Cover Photo: Elmina Castleby Kwabena Agyepong

Contents

"We know in a fashion which was not possible years ago what Africa believes, and where is the meeting place between our christian faith and the faith of the animist. What once was condemned as evil may today be recognised as rational, and not necessarily opposed to the Spirit of Christ."

From a letter by Dr Ephraim Amu in 1933, quoted in *Amu the African* by Fred Agyemang, Accra, 1988, p.89.

Acknowledgements

Every writer is in debt to those whose books he read and to those who helped him to understand his theme better. In my case, the names of former colleagues at PTC Akropong always come to mind. Those whose books taught me much and those who, in conversation and discussion clarified my understanding of Akan life and belief. I mention only a few: L.S.G.Agyemfra, F.Agyemang, C.A.Akrofi, C.G.Baeta, H.T.Dako, H.Debrunner, R.O.Danso, S.T.Akunor, J.H. Nketia, F.A.Gyampo, O.A.Boateng, A.L.Kwansa. Half a century later I still appreciate their friendship and fellowship.

My warmest thanks are due to Dr Margot Schantz for her constant encouragement and help as well as in preparing the book for the press. The responsibility for any errors or omissions, and for any expressions of opinion are mine.

For Cornelia and Frithjof

Foreword

Half a century ago when, as a young expatriate member of the teaching staff of the Presbyterian Training College, Akropong, Ghana, I experienced the kindness and the friendship of my colleagues and the people, it became abundantly clear to me, as never before, that skin colour had nothing to do with personality and character. Africans have no prejudice towards palefaces, as the American Indians called Europeans. I often felt ashamed, however, that my forbears, on the contrary, possessed a racial bias against people of another skin pigmentation. During the last four centuries the merchants of the sea-going nations of Europe, the Portuguese, the Spaniards, the British, the Dutch, the Danes and the Brandenburgers had engaged in the slave trade; they had bought Africans, shackled them in chains in their forts, transported them to the West Indian islands and the the Americas in the miserable holds of their ships, to sell those who survived the voyage in the slave markets to plantation owners. The survivors, for the rest of their lives, had to grow and harvest the cotton, the tobacco, the coffee and the sugar that Europeans had grown so fond of! This fate was not that of a small number. In the centuries from 1450 to 1900, slave exports amounted to more than eleven million human beings; an enforced out-sourcing and globalisation on the largest possible scale!

I often felt distressed to think that for so long a period this sordid business had continued and that even today, long after the abolition of slavery many of the palefaces of the world still consider those members of the human race whose skin hue is darker, to be inferior in every way to themselves, although we all belong to the same species *homo sapiens* and possess the same genetic structure. The enforced migration of this huge number of human beings to the so-called New World mainly from western Africa was a global catastrophe whose effects are still being felt.

I began to read widely about Ghana's history and the religion and philosophy of its people. Dr. J.B.Danquah's Akan doctrine of God led me to realise that the incorporation of certain major Akan insights into the Christian scheme had not yet taken place. I was struck by Dr. K.Aggrey's succinct analogy of the keys of the piano to illustrate the fact that, inevitably, blacks and whites must learn to live and work together: "You can play a tune on the white keys alone and on the black keys alone but for proper melody you need both." My colleague, Dr. C.A.Akrofi taught me the Twi of Akuapem and introduced me into the deeply interesting world of the Akan language with its proverbs and nuances. The first detailed *History of the Gold Coast and Ashanti* had come from the pen of C. Reindorf in 1889! Professor K.A.Busia had written his social survey of Sekondi-Takoradi and *The position of the Chief in Ashanti*. The Basel missionary J.G.Christaller had completed his monumental *Dictionary of the Asante and Fante Language* while R.S.Rattray had published his famous books on Ashanti, its Law and its Art and Religion.

I thought often about the relationship of Akan religion to Christianity and of the advice given to those who preached to the Anglo-Saxons in Britain over a thousand years ago "that they should tell their tidings of hope and salvation simply, to insist only on the essentials of faith and baptism, and to avoid anything that might needlessly offend the traditions of the people they had come to save. Christianity should be presented as the correction rather than the denial of their beliefs."

It seemed to me to be the reason why, when Akans accept Christianity they do not completely abandon their cherished, long-lived traditional customs and convictions. Out of this background, after a long interval, emerged my story, *It Happened in Ghana*.

Of course, most of the characters I have written about, apart from those who belong to the history books, never existed in real life; some of the names of towns and villages have been invented, they are a product of my imagination, But the advantage of a historical romance is that these fictitious characters lived and worked in a particular real and factual period in Gold Coast/Ghana history and this period gave me a framework for the story. During this period, many events, with far-reaching consequences, took place; everywhere people were trying to adjust to a rapidly-changing world; economic changes affected the lives of everyone. The historical facts are indisputable; how personal lives were lived at the time is the realm of the story-teller!

Noel Smith, Koenigstein Ts. Germany, Dec.2005.

1
Chapter

❧ *Afua Danso* ❧

The Asantehene remarked: "The white men who go to
Council with your master, and pray to the great God for
him, do not undertand my country, or they would not say
the slave trade is bad. But if they think it bad now, why did
they think it good before?"

British Consul and Envoy, Joseph Dupuis in his *Journal of a Residence in
Ashantee*, London, 1824.

It was in the middle of January 1824 that the news
reached Sir Charles McCarthy at Cape Coast Castle that
an Ashanti army of 10,000 men was advancing south to
punish the Denkyira tribe, whose chief, KojoTsibu, had
proposed leaving the Ashanti Confederation. The army also
planned to deal with the English who had raised and trained
a small local defence militia. They had halted to re-group at
the river Bonsa which flows into the Ankobra after passing
through Wasaw and Denkyira territory. Sir Charles doubted
that the enemy had advanced so near. Although he had read

Bowdich's renowned book, *A Mission to Ashantee*, published in 1819, which had reported fully on the wealth and organisation of the inland kingdom and the warlike capacity of its army he remained sceptical. His doubt and his incompetence led to utter defeat in the ensuing battle and cost him his life.

Afua Danso, a young girl of fifteen from the fishing village of Morree had accompanied her uncle to the battle front. He was a fisherman who had been recruited to the Fanti defence militia and as they marched they were preceded by the corps band until they reached the east bank of the river directly opposite the massed Ashanti warriors on the other side. Following the militia were three of the Fanti Asafo companies, one from Enyan Abaasa, one from Koromantine and her favourite Number 6 Company from Morree with large and small birds on their flag with the motto, "Birds of a feather flock together," a symbol of solidarity. It was all so exciting and no one imagined that the battle would end so tragically. Afua stood in the shade of a towering odum tree fom where she could see both banks of the river. As far as she could make out, from left to right, on a broad front, the soldiers of the enemy, each man equipped with a musket, cartridge belt round the waist, knives in girdles,some with swords and shields, had taken up their pre-arranged positions. Meanwhile, the horns of each chief by which the fighting groups were identified were blown and soon the traditional battle position of the Ashanti army was established: the main body in the middle flanked by the right and left wings so that at the crucial moment in the battle a pincer movement could take place and the enemy be surrounded.

At this point the river was about fifteen metres wide and it was clear that at places where there were sandbanks, the river could be forded. The prospects for the heavily outnumbered Fanti and British troops were not good.

Then, astonishingly, the militia band began to play the British national anthem, "God Save the King", and in the intervals the buglers played army calls like reveille and curfew and other signals. Perhaps, thought Afua, the white man believed that this music would induce the Ashantis to call a truce, she didn't know, but soon in defiant reply the talking drums boomed out: first the *ntumpane* and then the *fontomfrom*. She listened keenly: first came the taunt: *Yensuro wo, na yesoro hwan?* (If we don't fear you, whom do we fear?) Then came the ominous challenge: *Yema yenko nkofa Fante mesom.* (Lets go and bring Fanti to serve us), and after that the arrogant insult was heard: *Yema yenko nkofwe okurufa, na okurufa behu amane.* (Let's go and look for the rat and then the rat will be in real trouble). Each drummer sounded the sentence out on his own drum as a solo then all the drums roared out in unison until the forest itself resounded and reverberated. There was a dead silence broken only by the English command to fire as the Ashantis attempted to cross the river. They were repulsed a number of times but still the enemy persisted and Afua remembered the well-known saying about the bravery of the Ashanti warriors: *Wokum apem, okofo mpem edu reba*, (If you kill a thousand, ten thousand warriors take their place). There were no cowards, no one ran away or fell back. No one on the English side seemed to be aware that during the frontal attack the right and left wings of the enemy were fording the river lower down and higher up so as to be able to make flank attacks.

The frontal action went on until the English militiamen had used up all their ammunition and then the Ashantis gave the signal for an all-out attack on the militiamen from all sides who could now only defend themselves with bayonets. Afua watched horrified as group after group of the militia were surrounded and slaughtered: she saw her uncle killed and witnessed the last stand of Sir Charles McCarthy and three of his captains who fought with their backs to a large tree until they were overwhelmed; their heads were cut off to be taken as trophies to Kumasi. More than half of the militia force was killed and the rest was taken prisoner. It was the end of the Mankata campaign.

Akua had fallen down on her knees hoping to escape notice but suddenly a powerful bloodied arm seized her from behind, lifted her to her feet and turned her round. The warrior saw that she was a young girl, called her, *odonko ba* - slave girl – and motioned her to precede him down the bush path to the river bank where the prisoners of war were cross-ing. He gave her his skin bag which contained some dried plantain and cassava to carry, each soldier had to feed himself. She knew that she would be made a slave but she was not afraid because she also knew that a soldier who dared to have sexual intercourse with a captive girl would suffer a serious penalty; she belonged now to the chief of this man's company and all booty, human or otherwise, had to be declared.

In any case she had no real home; she lived as an orphan in her uncle's house and to be given as a slave in an Ashanti family would be no worse than in Morree and could, perhaps, be better. Domestic slaves in Ashanti could own property and even marry but, of course, they remained the possession of the head of the family and could even be sold or pawned. After a week of walking along well-trodden forest paths with little food or water she was duly presented to the chief of Bekwai who, in turn, gave Afua into the possession of his nephew, her captor, Kwame Asare Bafo, a sub-chief of an outlying village. The family was pleased to have her as a helper for all household duties: for the first time in her life she had enough to eat; she was given a mat to sleep on in a room with the children; she was given a new cloth to wear which had a strip of real silk kente in it and in the corner of the cloth she carefully knotted the small brass spoon which had been given to her at her puberty ceremony along with her waist beads and new loin cloth. The spoon had now become her special *suman* or personal charm and so long as she possessed it she felt comforted.

Her new-found security was not to last long; in her second year with the family she overheard her master talking to one of his sisters: she was to be sold outright in payment of a debt incurred by Bafo following the expenses of a family funeral. The money was owed to Santi, one of the biggest traders in Anomabu who owned a large shed in which were stored imported liquor, cotton-prints, silks, beads, bowls, muskets, gunpowder, ammunition, tobacco and pipes which the Ashanti paid for in gold dust and slaves. Dealing and trading in slaves in British ships had been abolished in 1807 but the Americans still continued importing them and Santi acted secretly as middleman. The Ashanti king had complained bitterly to the British consul Dupuis at Cape Coast: "If you think the slave trade bad now, why did you think it good before?"

Thus, a few days later, Afua found herself standing before

Santi while he assessed her price as a slave; she was young,strong and healthy, her light cocoa-coloured skin glowed like satin, her facial features were regular: small ears, a straight nose, a smile that showed good teeth, crinkly hair that had grown bushy but was trimmed around her ears and nape, warm brown eyes; her body was slender above long thighs, her breasts even and rounded, but her most attractive feature was her fine graceful neck, among African women the most coveted attribute. Her master, Asare Bafo had put her price high, and remarked, "The planters in America will pay much for such a girl; she is free from tribal marks and scars and will make a good house slave for domestic duties. She is worth five *pereguans* of gold not to speak of the children she may bear." His debt with interest had reached 32 sterling pounds; one English gold sovereign was worth 8 pounds sterling because it contained exactly one ounce of gold and if he could get at least four pereguans for the girl as well as a credit sum on his account he would have made a good bargain. He waited keenly for Santi's response.

The bargaining went slowly as always in Africa. Santi was wily and spoke of the size of the debt, of the cost of the girl's keep until an American ship anchored off-shore although he knew that with a girl like Afua he would easily cover his expenses. All the same, the risks had grown: the British were increasingly hostile to slave-handling and strict secrecy had to be maintained. The haggling continued until they agreed that six pereguans would cover the debt and expenses of the sale of Afua and that Bafo would be given one pereguan of credit in goods from the store, and one pereguan of gold dust. It was finally clear to Afua that she would be shipped across the wide ocean to the United States of America. She had previously thought that she would be pawned as a guarantee for the debt and perhaps later redeemed. It was a perennial problem in Akan society, ready cash was seldom available; a sub-chief like Asare Bafo could be quite rich in possessions and yet have difficulty in getting cash together to pay off a debt incurred by a family funeral or a wedding, so you bought on credit or you paid in kind or in services with help from your *abusua* (kindred group), or you could pawn a slave or even a member of your family. A trader like Santi who did business with the white man was one of the few who possessed cash and readily negotiable goods.

Afua watched while Santi produced the gold dust from a leather bag where it was kept in a small metal container. He took it a little at a time, placed it on a blow-pan, and skilfully puffed the dust particles away through a reed. A small nugget the size of a dried pea he cut in half with a sharp knife, rubbed the halves on a touchstone and examined the colour of the streaks with great care. He then weighed the gold with small weights cast into forms of human beings, animals, birds and geometrical designs to Bafo's satisfaction even though he had brought his own weights. Most chiefs carried a selection of these weights in a leather bag so that the two parties to the deal could check the amount of gold dust with their own weights. In conclusion, Bafo and Santi drank palm wine together, pouring out a little on the ground in reverence to the ancestors, and Afua became Santi's property.

After a week in a stifling dark shed near the shore listening to the regular beat of the pounding surf, Afua along with four other women and two children, were taken by canoe just before daybreak through the high-swelling, foam-capped waves to a two-masted schooner which was lying at anchor.

They had waited on the shore until the land breeze made it a bit easier to get through the surf. At the ship they were hauled in slings out of the bobbing boat onto the deck and from there into a cubby-hole in the hold: a small space enclosed by a metal grating through which they could see and smell the wooden casks of palm-oil, casks of fresh drinking-water, sacks of limes and vegetables and maize, while half-a-dozen fowls and two goats were tethered in a corner. They were given food twice a day, a piece of dried fish, a piece of plantain and a few groundnuts, maize flour made into a ball called kenkey, and water to drink. The women slaves were allowed to wander about on deck during the day in fine weather; the price they paid for this privilege was often to satisfy the sexual appetites of the crew. Afua was chosen by the third mate who had charge of the slaves to share his bunk in the stern whenever he was off duty. In fact, because his cabin was so small, they lay together in the boatswain's store where all the reserve ship's rigging was kept, making a mattress for themselves out of the folded linen sails. All she knew was that the name of the third mate was Bob and that he was a kind of sub-chief on the ship; he was tall and strong, lively and energetic, with light reddish hair tied in a ponytail. He wore a peaked naval cap, a thick grey flannel shirt and corduroy trousers held at the waist by a thick leather belt and a dark blue waist-length woollen pea-jacket. Bob took her under his wing; no other seaman was allowed to speak to her and whenever he was off-duty he came to her.

Afua had never lain with a man before but she was not unfamiliar with what was expected to take place; what surprised and delighted her was the tenderness that Bob showed before he entered her; the way he fondled and caressed her; the way he cradled her in his arms all of which showed her that he had a special regard for her. She marvelled at the smooth creaminess of his skin, only his face and hands and neck were ruddy because of exposure to the weather; she knew now why the white man was called *oburoni* in her language because *oburo* was the word for maize and that was exactly the colour of his skin. And in turn Bob marvelled at the light-brown silkiness of her skin like the milky cocoa he so enjoyed drinking, the poise of her head above her slender neck, her firm round breasts, her tempting hips and her long slim legs. All these roused him as never before. Never before had he experienced the sheer captivating beauty of the female form; white women were so overdressed that you never saw more than a pair of ankles or a hint of bosom, nothing much more. He was not married and with Afua he was overcome with a deep wave of tenderness towards her that he could not express in words, even if she could have understood English. But without words, the affection they felt for each other grew daily. Bob never stopped wondering at the miracle: she was a slave girl, being bought and sold for money yet she was every bit as refined and cultured as any white woman.

Every day he taught her new words in English: commonly-used verbs, names of different parts of the body and of white man's clothes; names for the different parts of the ship, names of food and drinks. It delighted her to learn that the ship was called *Nancy* because it reminded her of the Ananse stories that she had heard as a child. Ananse was the spider-hero of many Akan folk tales told to children around the evening fireside. Kweku Ananse indulged in all kinds of adventures which often landed him in disgrace, but he was clever and shrewd and always found a way out of tight corners. Bob also taught her to count in English with dried peas; he wrote out the English alphabet for her on a scrap of paper and she learned it by heart.

No man, not even her uncle, had shown her such consideration: he brought her extra tit-bits, sometimes tea with a dash of rum, sometimes scraps of cooked meat, sometimes a slice of white bread with jam on it, and they would laugh together as they ate. At other times he brought her an extra pail of fresh, sweet water to bathe with; he never tired of watching her wash herself and later, after they had made love, she would caress his face where his soft beard grew and nestle her head on the fuzz on his chest. One day he came with some palm oil and massaged her body while she gazed at him with wonder in her eyes.

For the first time in his life Bob began to think objectively about the slave trade: he was utterly captivated by a negro slave girl; a 'darky' as they called them in America, and 'darkies' were considered to be primitive, ignorant, lazy, dirty, by no means as far advanced as the whites, certainly inferior to them, only fit for hard labour in the fields and for menial tasks. But Afua was as good-looking as any white woman, she was modest even without clothes, friendly, good-humoured and intelligent, in the short time of a few weeks she had begun to ask questions in quite passable English. She was now able to explain to him in simple words something of her former life in the Gold Coast, how she had left her fishing village of Morree and had accompanied her uncle to Cape Coast and how she had been captured by the Ashantis at the battle of Asamanko during the Mankata campaign and had later been sold as a slave. Bob began fervently to hope that she would be bought by a good plantation owner and that she would be given domestic work in the homestead.

Before the ship landed the Captain gave the order to polish the slaves up, the better they looked the more they fetched at auction and the more his commission would be. Cuts, sores and abrasions were treated, some outward signs of illness and disease were covered up. They would, of course, be sold at auction naked apart from a loin-cloth so that they could be closely prodded and examined before the bidding began. Slaves were always sold singly so that children were often separated from their mothers and wives from husbands.

The last night before they reached port they sat on deck and talked; he told her that his real name was Robert Mason and that he came from Boston, a big city on the coast where they built ships and where settlers from England had landed. He was not married, his mother was a widow, he had two younger brothers and a sister and he was the sole support of the family. As the ship moved slowly up the James River, Afua could see lights on land and then as dawn broke, the harbour of Richmond, the capital city of the state of Virginia. He had tried to explain to her what would happen at the auction sale and how her new owner would take her to work on a big farm, either in the cotton or in the tobacco fields or in the large house of the owner and his wife. Bob realised now that he had become so fond of her that he would have liked to bid for her himself had he had money enough.

But every dollar he earned was needed by his widowed mother simply for the upkeep of the family. He embraced her for the last time and pressed into her hand an English gold sovereign to keep in her *ntama* together with the metal spoon that she had shown him.

In Richmond the crew and officers had two days' leave and at the right time Robert mingled with the onlookers at the docks where the slave auction traditionally took place. The bidders were mainly plantation owners or their foremen who were looking for strong males; others were seeking domestic slaves, mostly women, for household duties, cooks, housemaids, seamstresses and nursemaids, but Robert knew only too well that often life for the uprooted slave could be harsh and distressing.

The auctioneer was skilled: he had kept Afua to the last and then without saying a word he had taken her hand and paraded her in front of the spectators. There were audible expressions of surprise and admiration; Afua was beautiful by any standards, even unclothed she possessed a graceful-ness and a dignity which made the fashionable dresses of some of the women look tawdry by comparison. The bidding was brisk but the auctioneer was in no hurry to conclude the sale and then Robert understood, he had been waiting for the arrival of the Hazelwood brougham. Two well-dressed women descended from it, one a young woman of about seventeen, the other middle-aged. The Hazelwood family was one of the leading families of Virginia; who had not heard of Hazelwood Gold Leaf cigars and cigarettes and their sea-island cotton in such great demand in Europe? If only Afua could be bought by that family! Bob thought, as the germ of a plan began to course through his mind: he would give up his career at sea, make his way to Hazelwood and seek a job there.

The elder woman had taken one look at Afua and had

joined in the bidding; each time the auctioneer seemed to be about to close the bidding she made a higher bid and finally at a record price, Afua became Hazelwood property. She was warmly wrapped in a blanket and as soon as the payment formalities had been completed she was driven away in the coach. Robert stood still as the crowd dispersed, deep in thought; his heart was heavy because with Afua he had experienced a relationship with a woman whom he knew he might never find again. Not only that, she may well be carrying his child and that he had to know. Robert was not the sort of man to father a bastard with equanimity, even with a negro slave girl. He was sorry to see her go but he was satisfied that she would belong to a good family. There were good and bad owners; some were bad-tempered and a few were downright cruel but Hazelwood had a good reputation. Henry Harwood Hazelwood was the second son of a Liverpool textile merchant and had been sent out by his father with three thousand pounds to grow long-staple sea-island cotton. That was in 1795 and in thirty years he had built up a great estate centred on a large luxurious mansion, the homestead. On the estate was a village for the slave workers; there were barns, workshops, stables, vegetable and fruit gardens, a dairy farm together with all the equipment and materials of a landed aristocrat in nineteenth century England. He was a hard-working, hard-living and hard-headed cash-crop farmer whose word was law. He was considered to be 'soft' towards blacks but he did not hesitate to use the whip against recalci-trant workers and thieves and against all those who neglected their duties, and especially against violence and drunkenness. His grudging compassion towards his slaves was due in part to his recognition that without them he would have achieved little; in part from his wife and cousin Dorcas, who had sailed from Liverpool to marry him and had brought with her strong views on the abolition of slavery. She had recognised the position in the southern states but had worked tirelessly on the plantation to ameliorate the situation of the slaves; they were properly fed, their houses were kept in repair, there was a school for the children with a black teacher and the families were given allotments on which they could grow vegetables or keep pigs or poultry.

Afua became the personal maidservant of Rebecca the only child of the Hazelwoods and she confided her pregnancy to Dorcas who saw that she was cared for until her son was born. A black Baptist preacher conducted the baptism at which the baby was given the name: Robert Danso Morree, the names of the father and the mother, together with the name of the fishing village on the Gold Coast where Afua had been born. But although the father was a native-born citizen of the United States, baby Robert was classed as a slave. Yet these years were comfortable ones for Afua and her mulatto son: she learned to speak English like educated white people, she learned sewing, cooking, housekeeping; she became Rebecca's close companion and friend and increasingly filled the role of trusted and confidential servant. Robert was sent to school in Richmond and later became head groom in charge of the horses and overseer of the harvesting, curing and transport of the tobacco as well as the shipping of the cotton. Afua and her son moved up in status and were given rooms in the main house and given a role to play as an accepted part of the family yet they were still officially categorized as slaves! They overheard discussions about politics, how there were states in the north where the blacks were free to lead their own lives and there were those who argued that slavery in the southern states should be abolished. Hazelwood was strongly of the view that each state should decide its own policy on slavery. The argument between the northern and the southern states on this topic went on interminably until a number of the southern states seceded from the Union and formed a Confederation with its own President and capital in Richmond. On the morning of the 12th April 1861 the first shots were fired in a bloody civil war during which half a million men were to lose their lives.

The slaves at Hazelwood and on all the plantations were in a ferment, they knew that if the northern Union army won the war they would be free but no one was sure about this until after the dreadful three-day battle at Gettysburg in Pennsylvania in July 1863. In the November of that year a portion of the battlefield was dedicated as a final resting place for those men of both armies who had been killed there and President Lincoln's final words in his short speech made it quite clear that all men and women in the United States would be equal and free. The speech marked the turning-point of the war, it seemed certain now that the Union would win. Reuben, the spokesman for the Hazelwood slaves asked Dorcas for a meeting at which he produced a tattered and soiled sheet of paper.

"Tell us, Missus, what all this means? It says at the top, 'Lincoln is the slaves' only hope'. We don't know what is happening and what we shall do." Dorcas read the last sentence of Lincoln's address aloud: "... we here highly resolve that these dead shall not have died in vain, that this nation, under God, shall have a new birth of freedom, and that government of the people, by the people, for the people, shall not perish from the earth." It means that in the United States all men and women are equal and free; all people shall have the same rights.

"Are we people, Missus ? We slaves, I mean?"

"Yes. If the north wins the war you will have the same rights as whites, you will be citizens with a vote. You will be able to travel and live and work where you like."

"If we go away what will happen to Hazelwood?"

"I don't know how it will work out, Reuben, that will be a matter for the Master to decide when he comes back from the war."

"When will the Master come back, Missus?"

"He has sailed to England to try to get help to beat the blockade. There are many unemployed there because they cannot buy our cotton. He will return soon."

There was some further discussion after which they decided to stay on the plantation until the return of Mr Hazelwood.

After the battle of Gettysburg the war continued but inevitably the overwhelming superiority in man-power, material supplies and money proved to be decisive; the armies of Grant and Sherman advanced up the Mississippi valley from New Orleans, Richmond itself was twice attacked and finally in November 1864 northern forces marched from Atlanta to Savannah and cut the southern forces in two, the civil war was over, the nation was re-united and the slaves were free.

But what could the slaves do? Most of them were untrained agricultural labourers who were illiterate and without any experience of social life outside the plantation. Some of the younger single men joined the army, others became small tenant farmers and share-croppers when the plantation system came to an end. Those who tried their luck in the wider world had to be content with menial employment. Many bundled their few belongings together and trekked north to Washington or to Philadelphia or to large towns in states where slavery did not exist. In the southern states after the war there was very little attempt to integrate former slaves into the white community and the blacks formed a permanently depressed social group.

A few days later Afua sought Robert out at the stables, she had to talk to him about their future plans. He had finished exercising the black stallion, Danny, the one they used for breeding and now he was grooming him. It wasn't his horse, of course, but he rode it the most and there was a close relationship between the two of them. Afua loved the powerful horse scent and the acrid, earthy reek of the stables. She felt young still and in the twenty years that she had lived and worked at Hazelwood she had learned much of the ways of the living and thinking of the whites. How lucky she had been to have been bought by Hazelwood, how fortunate to have had Dorcas as a mistress! Yet how smug and unfeeling towards Africans the vast majority of whites could be, as though to be born with a white skin was an automatic claim to superiority; even the poor whites demonstrated this attitude. She had heard many tales of the cruelty of harsh masters on other plantations; every slave had bitter personal tales to tell of rapes and floggings with a rawhide whip, of girls and women hired out as prostitutes and of the brutal discipline of males, the so-called 'seasoning' in the fields for bad work or laziness when they were forced to work without rest from dawn to dusk or even through the night if time was pressing to dig, hoe, weed, plough, or to collect grass for the horses and cattle. If you were late you could be whipped and put on short rations and you had no redress, no one to appeal to. The only consolation for most of the slaves was on Sundays and on the occasional day's holiday when they listened to a travelling Baptist or Methodist revivalist preacher or worked on their allotments and there would be singing, drumming and dancing African-style. And such heartfelt singing! There would be someone who would suddenly cry out, after hearing the story of the prophet Elijah's journey to heaven in the chariot of fire; "Swing low, sweet chariot, coming for to carry me home." Or after hearing the story of the entry of the Israelites into the land of Canaan across the Jordan river, "When the saints go marching in… I wanna be in that number…," and everybody would join in, singing and handclapping, a great harmony of longing and yearning.

And now that this terrible war had come and whites were killing one another in thousands so that slavery would be abolished in all the states and blacks would be free citizens like the whites; but would that ever really happen?

Robert looked up from his grooming and they sat down together on a bench, he knew that she wanted to talk.

"What are we, you and me, going to do when this war is over?" she asked.

"If the south loses the war we shall be free to go away and I think that we should go north somewhere."

"I believe so too. I have heard Dorcas talk about a state called Pennsylvania in the north where there is no slavery, where there are many whites who believe in living and working together in peace. We came from Africa but we can't go back there, somehow we have to live as Americans among American people. But first we must wait until the war is over and get our citizenship papers."

Then one day in late January 1865, a solitary man on horseback arrived at the Hazelwood homestead and requested an interview with the owner. He was shown into Mr Hazelwood's study where a grey-haired and grey-bearded old man greeted him courteously.

"I am informed that you wish to speak with me."

"My name is Robert Mason from Boston, Massachusetts, recently discharged from the United States Navy. Twenty years ago I was third mate of the brig *Nancy* which brought a cargo of slaves from the Gold Coast to Richmond. One of those slaves was a girl called Afua Danso with whom, strange as it may sound, I fell in love. I saw her purchased at auction by a lady from Hazelwood. My plan was to give up the sea and to find employment in Richmond but events overtook me; I returned to Boston to find my widowed mother seriously ill; my two younger brothers and a sister became my responsibility. From then on I signed on for only short voyages. My mother never fully recovered her health and died just before the civil war broke out; I was drafted into the Navy and attained the rank of captain.

"Only now upon my discharge have I been free to come to Hazelwood and to enquire about the slave Afua Danso. I think that it is possible that Afua was pregnant by me and I am much concerned to know if that was indeed the case."

"You have a fine son, Captain Mason, who bears your first name. He is employed on the estate to look after the horses and the transport, he is at the moment in Richmond on business. Afua is our housekeeper."

"Did she ever marry?"

"No. My wife and I believed that she was always loyal to her memory of you. But I should like my wife to hear all this astonishing news. Let me call her."

When Dorcas appeared Hazelwood said:

"My dear, this fine young man, Captain Mason, claims to be Robert's father. How shall he convince us?"

"He should tell us something about Afua that no one else could possibly know, even something that we don't know."

Bob thought quickly, what could he possibly mention?

"Did Afua ever tell you about what she always kept carefully tied in one corner of her Gold Coast cover cloth, the one with the Ashanti silk kente stripe in it?"

"She may have told Rebecca but she never said anything to us."

"Then I know what she keeps hidden there; an Ashanti brass spoon which was given to her at puberty and an English gold sovereign which I gave to her the night before we landed at Richmond."

"That is enough for us, Dorcas can mention it privately to her. You know, Captain Mason, we have grown very fond of Afua and we are delighted to learn that you have come to claim her. Dorcas, please ask Afua to join us."

As soon as Afua entered the room it was clear to Henry Hazelwood that as Afua's eyes rested on Captain Mason there was no shadow of doubt about the naval officer's claim. She stood quite still, tears began to roll down her cheeks and then suddenly she held out her arms to him and said:

"Bob, at last you have come back to me!"

Then the two were locked in a tight embrace and as they

slowly drew apart Afua exclaimed proudly, "Your son Robert is tall and strong like you with your eyes and hair!"

Bob, still holding one of Afua's hands in his, turned to Hazelwood and spoke with great feeling.

"I should like, sir, to spend some time here with you if you can offer me employment and allow me to marry Afua. Like most mariners, I am a useful handyman, I could assist with shipping and transport problems, and I should welcome the opportunity to get to know my son. Then, when things have settled down I should be grateful for your permission to take them away to the north to start a new life."

"That is only fair. Give us a little of your help, Captain Mason. You are aware how things are after the war: the era of the plantation system is over but we have to organise in a different way; the cotton and the tobacco still have to be grown and sold to produce revenue to rebuild our shattered country. We are feeling our way slowly towards a new system; many of my former slaves are prepared to work for me for wages. I have had to make a large slice of the estate available to independent share-croppers and I'm slowly re-establishing our export links with Europe. But it will all take time and Virginia is now poor and devastated by war. The carpet-baggers and the do-gooders from the north are everywhere. I shall be grateful for all the help you can give me."

Thus it was that Bob moved into Hazelwood and he and his son began to play a leading part in the organisation of the estate while Dorcas and Afua took care of the household. There was a never-to-be-forgotten celebration week-end during which Afua and Bob were married after Afua and Robert had received their citizenship papers; all three were united as an American family and they looked forward to a new life together in the future in one of the northern states. Afua was convinced that a life in Pennsylvania offered them the most attractive prospects and almost three years after the end of the war they set off on their journey. Hazelwood and Dorcas were really sorry to see them leave but they were also grateful for all that the Mason family had done to help them; the stallion, Danny, was given to Robert, and Bob and Afua were presented with mounts and a mule to carry their few possessions; in addition each had a hundred dollars. They kept away from the main highways and travelled slowly, buying provisions in the villages and often sleeping in the open. Although the war was over, blacks on the move north met some unfriendliness; the idea that emancipated slaves could now travel freely was difficult for some whites to accept. One day they reviewed their plans.

"Why are we heading for Pennsylvania?" asked Bob.

"Because I have been told that many of the whites there are different," replied Afua.

"How different?" Bob wanted to know.

"Pennsylvania state was founded by a man called William Penn who was the leader of a Quaker group and they called their capital town Philadelphia, a name which means brotherly love. They just wanted to live in peace and harmony with everybody, including Indians and blacks, what colour your skin was didn't matter at all. Then groups from Europe with similar ideas like the Mennonites and Amish people started to move in. Dorcas told me about them, they are all Christians who believe in living humbly and modestly like Jesus, in peace and friendliness with everybody; they don't fight or do military service, they try always to speak the exact truth, they don't need to swear oaths, they oppose slavery and they all work on the land. I should very much like to meet people like that and maybe settle among them; our roots in Africa have almost all withered away, so we need to put new roots down somewhere in America, perhaps where we can find work on a farm. Dorcas suggested going through Washington, then Philadelphia and after that head west to Lancaster County where many of these people are settled."

"How shall we know when we get there? I mean where these people actually live?" asked Robert.

"From what I have been told these people dress in black. The women wear black bonnets and capes, the men wear dark jackets and trousers, black broad-brimmed hats and all grow beards. They are all farmers who live in close family groups and who make most of the things they need themselves from natural materials. The German groups use that language at home and at church services but they all speak English. The Quakers came from England but William Penn invited the others from Germany; they love horses and every boy receives a horse on his fourteenth birthday to work with on the land."

They travelled through gently rolling hills, wooded valleys, and pasture land until they reached the city of Philadelphia built along the Delaware River where hundreds of freed slaves were to be seen. In reply to their questions they were directed to Germantown a few miles north through which the religious groups had originally entered the country. On their way west in the direction of Lancaster they had stopped overnight by a copse through which a small stream flowed, there was abundant grass for the animals as well as shade and shelter under a large sycamore tree. To their astonishment a one-horse buggy drew up alongside and a lean broad-shoul-dered young man got out and greeted them.

"My name is Gottfried Thomas from Landis Valley, who may you be?"

Robert replied by introducing his wife and son.

"We are looking for work and a place to settle in Pennsylvania because we have heard good reports of the white people here," he continued.

"Have you any experience of farming?"

"I was a sea captain for many years and for the last three years I have assisted in the organisation of a large plantation near Richmond in Virginia; my son was head groom of 24 working horses and had the care of a small breeding stud. He has a wide experience in the care of horses: feeding, training, illnesses and such things. Danny, who is grazing over there is a Hanoverian, we used him for breeding but he's getting old now and Mr Hazelwood gave him to us as a parting present." Son Robert called Danny who nuzzled his shoulder over while Robert spoke in his ear. "I talk to him, sir, whenever there's anything new."

"Did your wife work on the farm?" Gottfried Thomas asked Bob.

"She worked often in the vegetable garden and in the orchard but her main duty was to be the personal maid of Rebecca, the daughter of the house, and later housekeeper. She learned to read and write, to cook and to sew as well as to look after the kitchen stores. My son Robert was three years at the boys' school in Richmond at the expense of Mr Hazelwood."

Gottfried was thinking furiously, he was on his way to Germantown to try to recruit a young immigrant and his wife to look after the livestock, the dairy and the household and by chance he had encountered this family Mason with their interesting history and background. Between them they possessed the qualifications he wanted badly for his farm, especially with horses; they spoke English well just like educated whites; they were all citizens of the United States and the wife had a long experience of running a large white household. His farm wasn't so big, about 500 acres, but he desperately needed experienced help to cope with the planned development of the farm and to support his wife and sister. But would they be in sympathy with Mennonite ideas and their way of life?

"I should tell you that in our district we live by what some people would call old-fashioned notions. We are simple believing Christians living sincerely and modestly in family groups in friendship and peace with all our neighbours. Every fourteen days we join with the other families in our district for the worship of God, we sing hymns and pray and listen to a sermon in the old German language and afterwards we join together and exchange our news and chat over our domestic affairs before we go back home. Would you consider coming to live and work on our farm? There is a large log cabin that you can have. You would take all your meals with us in the farmhouse and my wife and my sister would help you in every way to make your life comfortable. Any money that we earn by the sale of produce or of livestock is held in common, and if you join us you would each have a sixth share of any profits that we made."

Afua had listened carefully to the conversation between Bob and Gottfried. All that Gottfried had said bore out what Dorcas had told her about the religious groups in Pennsylvania and he himself had made an excellent impression of honesty and probity upon her. He and Robert were not so far apart in age and Robert's experience with horses had clearly made a favourable impact. The main thing, however, was that they were being accepted as equals by a white family and being given the opportunity to integrate themselves into an American community which had no prejudice against blacks. It really was as Dorcas had said, there were white people who tried to love their neighbour regardless of the colour of their skin. Bob had turned to her enquiringly and without discussion she had nodded and smiled her agreement. It was a happy moment as the four shook hands warmly and then began their journey together to Landis Valley. They loaded some of their baggage into the buggy and Afua took her seat by Gottfried, Robert mounted Danny while Bob rode his horse and led the mule. They made a halt in Lancaster to buy supplies before making their way finally to Landis Valley farm where they were warmly welcomed by Käthe, Gottfried's sister, and by Christa, his wife, who both immediately made them feel at home.

That was in the year 1868 nearly four years after the end of the civil war. The Mason family never became Mennonites but they felt contented to live and work among such people whose simple faith impressed them. Following the example of Jesus of Nazareth gave them a working rule – love your neighbour as yourself, be merciful and kind, honest and truthful, modest and steadfast, without getting involved in abstruse theological doctrines and formulations. It was an example that commended itself to Afua, Bob and Robert. So as in Hazelwood the three of them began to make an ever-increasing contribution to the life and work of the farm. Robert's skill with horses endeared him to the farmers in the district who brought their sick and disabled animals to him and, within the family he had awakened in Käthe an interest in horses.

Käthe was shy, retiring and self-conscious as a result of a disabled left arm after having suffered from poliomyelitis as a child. Robert had taught her to ride with complete assurance; she had become a competent horsewoman and shared with Robert the oversight of the livestock. So it was, that when Käthe and Robert were married in 1870, after the ceremony they found that the clerk in the Register Office had anglicised the name Morree to Morrow. They had two children, Paul Thomas Morrow and Roberta Nancy Morrow, and together with Gottfried and Christa's young son Werner the farmhouse was suddenly alive with the sound of children's voices and laughter.

Oma Afua (grandma Afua) was always in demand for stories from the Gold Coast about Ananse and about her life as a child in the fishing village of Morree where the children would gather on the beach at daybreak to see the canoes breast the huge surf waves and paddle furiously to shore and unload their catch in the nets; huge mounds of glistening and squirming fish of all sorts and sizes. The fish would be sorted there and then and sold to the market mammies and to other buyers. She never tired of telling how she had been captured by the Ashantis in 1824 and then sold as a slave. Before she died in 1900 – she was 81 years old then – she entrusted her small metal Ashanti spoon, her waist beads and her ntama cloth with the coloured silk stripe to Roberta Nancy Morrow, Robert's daughter.

"That is all I possess of my Gold Coast past life, don't let it be forgotten, pass them on to your children and grandchildren. Maybe one day one of them may want to go there and find out where Oma was born and lived as a girl."

Afua was beloved by all the families in the district for her gentleness and her winsomeness and for the wonderful way that she had overcome the handicap of being sold as a slave. Bob had died a few years earlier; he had also become a popular figure among the men for his profession as a sailor and for the yarns of the sea that he could tell. He became treasurer of the Thomas farm and he was often consulted by other families for his sound advice on planning and financing.

Roberta never married but her brother Paul's grand-daughter, Thelma Nancy Morrow, who was born in 1933, became the owner of Oma Afua's keepsakes. Her mother had also passed on to her the story of the romance with Bob on board the *Nancy* and how later after the end of the civil war the three of them had trekked north to Pennsylvania so that the mementos of Afua's early life acquired a special importance for her and awoke in her the desire to find out more about her ancestors in West Africa.

From time to time news filtered through from European newspapers of events in the Gold Coast, how finally the Dutch and the Danes had relinquished their forts leaving the British the sole European country with interests on the coast, and how in 1869 an Ashanti army had invaded Akwamu and had taken three Europeans hostage to Kumasi while another army had marched to Elmina. At length, Major-General Sir Garnet-Wolseley had been sent from Britain as Governor of the territory with a large body of troops. He had driven the Ashantis from the area south of the Pra river, pursued them as far as Kumasi which he totally destroyed. By a peace treaty at Fomena, the Ashantis undertook to maintain permanent peace, to pay an indemnity, to withdraw their forces from the south, to abandon all claims to Elmina, and to allow freedom of trade. This war of 1873-74 became known as the Sagrenti War, the Ashanti version of 'Sir Garnet'.

But the Ashanti problem was not yet, however, solved. Some of the tribes who made up the confederation began to declare their independence; there was no effective occupation by the British until in 1896 a British force marched unopposed to Kumasi where, in spite of the Asantehene's submission, he, the queen-mother, his father, his two uncles and his brother, together with a number of sub-chiefs, were taken prisoner, removed to Cape Coast and thereafter exiled to the Seychelles Islands.

Four uneasy years had ensued. The Ashantis were by no means reconciled to the loss of their leaders, and when Sir Frederick Hodson, the Governor, at a formal meeting with chiefs in Kumasi demanded the surrender of the Golden Stool, the chiefs retired in disgust and once again began decisive action which led to war. They besieged the Governor and his wife, some missionaries from Basel, twenty-four other European soldiers and civilians as well as 750 troops, in the fortress in Kumasi while thousands of refugees crowded beneath the walls. A request for military help could be sent before the single telephone line was cut, but the siege lasted for two months before fresh troops were able to relieve the garrison. The Ashanti army was split up into guerrilla bands which were defeated only with difficulty. Peace had been slowly established and in 1902 Ashanti had been formally annexed by the British. This war became known as the Yaa Asantewa war. Yaa was the queenmother of the town of Ejisu and she had inspired the chiefs to fight. She and fifteen other leaders were also deported to the Seychelles to join the Asantehene.

The demand for the surrender of the Golden Stool had been a great blunder. The stool is a low wooden seat carved out of one piece of wood according to a specific design and symbolises the identity, unity and continuity of the tribe and the entire community. Every paramount chief, clan chief, town or village head possesses a stool; 'to sit on the stool' not only indicates political power but at the same time the chief represents the ancestors and as such he links the living and the dead. The stool and all that it stands for is thus the 'soul' of the people and on festival days especially during the Odwira ceremony the stool is paraded through the town accompanying the chief. The Golden Stool of the Asantehene was the shrine and symbol of the national soul of the people; it was carried by the head stool-carrier upon the nape of his neck and sheltered from the sun by the great umbrella known as Katamanso (the covering of the nation). Since the war of 1900 the Golden Stool had been buried and to have given it up would have been felt as an ultimate desecration and humiliation.

Thelma, Afua's great-granddaughter grew up with a special interest in the Gold Coast. She had been fascinated by Afua's life story, from slave girl to honoured ancestress of the Morrow family, a story backed up by the brass spoon and the kente cover cloth. She began to read all that she could lay her hands on about the Gold Coast. Bowdich's *Mission to Ashantee* fascinated her with its detailed accounts of Ashanti social life and religion; Reindorf's *History of the Gold Coast and Asante*, the first African history written in 1895, and of course, Rattray's detailed volumes on *Religion and Art in Ashanti* and *Ashanti Law* written in the 1920s, the first real anthropological descriptions. Quite by chance, in a second-hand bookshop she found a copy of *West African Sketches* by A. B. Ellis dating from 1881 which was full of information about Fanti life in the area around Cape Coast and Morree where Afua was born. It all captivated her and strengthened her resolve one day to visit the Gold Coast.

What was clear from all her reading about the years between 1900 and 1957 during the British colonial time was that there had been astonishing progress in the country: roads, railways, harbours and administrative buildings had been constructed, thanks mainly to the Christian missions an educational system was in being as well as hospitals and clinics, industry and commerce had so far developed that the per capita income in the Gold Coast was second only to South Africa. Much of the wealth came from cocoa (about half the world's production), gold, mahogany and hardwoods, and palm oil. The cocoa was grown in clearings in the forest on plots between 5 and 10 acres by families; the large trees were left standing to provide shade for the cocoa trees. It was forbidden for foreigners to own land. The crop was marketed by European trading firms through the Cocoa Marketing Board which advanced cash to the farmer for half the estimated tonnage of the crop, the balance being paid at harvest. The 1950s marked the beginning of significant political developments away from colonial rule towards autonomy through a political party system and after 1951 the Convention People's Party set up by Kwame Nkrumah became the spearhead of constitutional change. When the party gained overwhelming support in the elections of 1956 the way was clear for the granting of full independence the date being fixed for the 6th March 1957. As the Gold Coast would be the first European colony in Africa to gain independence, world interest was aroused. The new name of Ghana was taken from the medieval kingdom of Ghana in the western Sudan on the assumption that the people of the Gold Coast are descendants of immigrants from the Ghana of the 11th century. So Thelma became really excited, she had Gold Coast blood in her veins inherited from Afua and after she had gained some experience of teaching she would volunteer for work in her great-grandmother's native land. That was the reason why in January 1958 she wrote a letter to the Peace Corps administrative office in Washington D. C. requesting an interview.

Chapter

Kwabena Opoku from Berekum, Ashanti, and his grandson Ben Berricombe.

"The enemy lay hiding in wait in the middle of what they call here 'bush', but should be more appropriately called a jungle,…. This is the bush into which the Ashanti warriors creep on all fours and lie in wait in the gloomy recesses for the enemy. It was in such a locality as this that Sir Garnet (Wolseley) found the Ashantis, and where he suffered such loss in his staff and officers."

Henry M. Stanley : *Coomassie and Magdala. The Story of Two British Campaigns in Africa.* London, 1874.

In the month of December, 1874, as the coast first appeared in the shape of a long, low, dark line on the northern horizon, officers and men of the troopship *Hermes* clustered at the ship's rail avid for their first glimpse of the Gold Coast, the land of slaves and gold, of malaria and blackwater fevers and of the redoubtable Ashanti warriors that they were pledged to drive out of the protectorate whatever the cost. The setting sun had formed a golden haze over the land but as the ship slowly drew nearer the watchers could discern a fringe of palms, a strip of gleaming white sand, the foam lines of the breakers and further inland a dense mass of forest-covered, low, undulating hills. On the sea side of the surf were several fishing canoes and the white sails of a patrolling gunboat were to be seen and by the time their ship had dropped anchor off Cape Coast the sun had set; the golden haze had been replaced by a kind of greyish mist above the thick vegetation while the outline of the castle had become blurred.

The thoughts of the soldiers on board were preoccupied with the dangers of the climate and with the fierce enemy they had to fight. The coast of West Africa was in itself a death-trap, it wasn't known as the 'white man's grave' for nothing; out of the misty vapour in an unknown way came a deadly infection by which you started shivering and sweating at the same time, you couldn't keep warm and yet you were bathed in your own sweat, then you passed out and when you woke the shaking and the sweating were repeated until you felt as weak as a baby and you had no appetite and you could scarcely drink. If there was no quinine available you had no chance at all of survival; your piss turned black, a sure sign that the fever had got a death-grip on you. You lost consciousness again and this time you never woke up. As if that wasn't enough, there was the enemy who fought only to win and who in four campaigns against the British had come out on top and who had reduced all the other tribes in the Gold Coast to servitude and whose discipline in battle was renowned. Although they only had old-fashioned flint-lock muskets they closed in on you out of the dark recesses of the forest so that suddenly you were surrounded on every side by black figures who moved with the speed of light and who hacked you to death with their long knives and spears. They resembled the soldier-ants which never halted but kept on attacking, however many you killed, until your own resistance came to an end. In battle no Ashanti ever ran away or stopped fighting or surrendered; he had sworn an oath to serve his king even to death and he advanced and fought until the enemy was totally subdued. After the pincer-movement of the army by which the enemy was completely encircled came the close combat. If the Ashantis had been armed with the breech-loading Snider rifles with sufficient ammunition, it is unlikely that the British would ever have defeated them.

Their sergeant had fought against Zulus in South Africa and the questions of the men were addressed to him.

"When do we go ashore, Sarge?"

"Probably at first light. The Kroomen will take us through the surf in canoes so make sure that all your personal gear is well-packed and secure."

"Where are the Ashanti troops? Do we have to fight them to get ashore?"

"No. They'll just observe us and when they see which way we intend to march they'll let us advance inland far enough not to be able to retreat to the castle and wait for us in a prepared position. You won't see them until they attack you."

"Do we form squares then, Sarge?"

"Yes, it's your only chance. Rapid fire, make every bullet tell; then back to reload. Any wounded man gets back into the square and fixes his bayonet. You all know the drill. If there is a defensive position you can get to in time, take it but wait for the order from me or the corporal. No one leaves the group.

Then you fight to the last man. Understood? If you can hold them off until dark the Ashantis will break off the attack because at night in the forest you can't see your hand in front of your face, it's absolutely pitch dark. They will retire to regroup and you will have the chance to do the same and join up with your comrades. It's them or us this time, we're here to teach them a lesson they will never forget."

In fact, the troops and all the equipment were landed without incident and the British advanced northwards by the normal track to Kumasi, a dirt road about three metres wide northwards through Nsuta and Fosu to the river crossing at Prasu. Near Fosu was fought one of the fiercest battles of the entire campaign. Kwabena Opoku, the nephew of the chief of Berekum, had been put in charge of the right-wing combat group with orders to break through the last British detachment bringing up the rear of the marching column which was a kilometre in length. This detachment of the Dorset Yeomanry was commanded by Captain Henry Horrocks. The track was barely wide enough for four men to march abreast; on their left was thick forest, to their right more open savanna-like terrain which led down to the Pra river. The marching troops were nervous, there had been no sign of the enemy since they had left Cape Coast four days ago. The villages that they had passed through had been completely deserted and the scouts had no information.

Then suddenly at a point where a small creek flowed into the Pra and the troops had to mark time while the creek was forded, a hail of musket fire met them and thousands of black warriors leapt out of their forest cover towards them. There was barely time to form squares along the track and the yeomanry in the rear formed the vulnerable left flank.

The rapid Snider rifle fire of the British halted the first centre attack of the Ashantis causing heavy casualties and there was stalemate on the right but the British left flank came under renewed intensive attack from three sides so that the square was broken and desperate hand-to-hand fighting ensued. Horrocks yelled the order for every man to fight his own way along the track to their comrades but their cohesion as a fighting unit had been lost and it was every man for himself. He himself followed a side track into the forest down which some of his men had run when he was brought down by a spear in his thigh. As his assailant caught up with him he just had time to draw his pistol and shoot him. All he remembered after that was crawling painfully to the shelter of an odum tree, removing the spear and trying to staunch the copious flow of blood from his wound with his shirt and to keep the ants and flies away and then he lost consciousness. He awoke some time later to find himself being carried across the shoulder of a man he took to be an Ashanti fighter and hoped that perhaps he had been taken prisoner and as an officer might possibly be ransomed; at least his head was still on his shoulders! From pain and loss of blood he fainted again and this time awoke to find himself on a camp-bed in the British army field hospital, standing over him was his commanding officer.

"You've been very lucky, Horrocks. Had you been found under other circumstances they would have cut your head off. How do you feel now? The surgeon says that your wound should fairly soon heal but the thigh muscle is damaged. We shall make arrangements to send you home by the next ship."

"Who brought me in?"

"Almost at nightfall the picket sentry spotted an Ashanti soldier carrying you across his shoulders, when he was challenged he waved a white cloth, the remains of your shirt. He seems to be some sort of an officer, he surrendered formally to us as prisoner of war and gave his name as Kwabena Opoku, a sub-chief from Berekum. I've called in an interpreter so that we can hear his story together. Are you feeling up to that?"

"Yes, I am. I am curious to know why one of the enemy should think that I was worth saving and then to surrender himself."

Kwabena Opoku, accompanied by a Fanti interpreter were shown into the tent. He held himself to attention, left arm at his side, right arm across his chest. He wore his ntama cover cloth over his left shoulder, his cartridge belt was around his waist and he had been allowed to keep his knife girdle for the interview. His demeanour was that of a man in authority; he was about one metre 90 tall and looked at the commanding officer with an intelligent and respectful look on his face as though to indicate that he recognised superior authority. In answer to the questions put to him through the interpreter he gave the following account of himself.

"I was born in Berekum, in the west of Ashanti region and as the nephew of the chief I was required to do service at the court of the Ashanti king in Kumasi. I was trained as a soldier and was recruited into the army to serve under the Mampong chief (the Nifahene), who in time of war assumes total command of all the armed forces. The Mampong regiment always forms the right wing of the army in battle. All soldiers swear an oath of allegiance, to fight to the death, never to surrender or to be captured. During the recent battle I was ordered to lead the combat troops of the right flank to break the British left defence square and to lead the attack to the rear of the British line. We almost succeeded but the white soldiers fought so fiercely with their fixed bayonets and pistols that my men could not begin the attack on the rear of the British line. Both sides were fighting man to man in all directions and it was clear to me that we had failed. I personally was involved in hand-to-hand combat and when I followed a group of British soldiers down a footpath I was suddenly alone and then I noticed this wounded British officer on the ground half-hidden in the bush.

"The officer was alive but unconscious and was bleeding from a spear wound in his right thigh, one of my comrades lay dead nearby. I decided there and then to desert from my comrades, to carry the officer to safety and to give myself up to the British as a prisoner of war. I knew that the British treated prisoners of war decently so my life would be spared. What was the reason for my decision? During my time at the king's court in Kumasi I had a love affair with one of the wives of the king. She was an Ewe woman taken captive during the campaign in the east and I would have liked to marry her but this was quite impossible and for a long time we met secretly. But among our people nothing can be kept secret for very long and one day a friend told me that the matter was known. I knew then that as soon as the information reached the ears of the king, protocol demanded that both she and I would be put to death even though I was the nephew of the chief of Berekum and his likely successor. I took the earliest opportunity to get her back to her people across the Volta River. She made the excuse of a death in the family and was allowed to go but it was not so easy for me to leave Ashanti. I was regularly at court and deeply involved in military affairs. You may not know that a man who has had sexual intercourse with one of the wives of the king is executed is in public by the prolonged, agonising *atopere* method. It starts with skewering his tongue so that he cannot swear the forbidden oath against the king, his shins are scraped, the testicles and penis are excised, ears and nose are cut off, then the feet, after which the victim, if he is still alive, is forced to walk on the stumps, all to the accompaniment of the ribaldry of the executioner and the bawdy comments of the spectators. You will understand, Sir, that although I am not a coward," he looked at the commanding officer with a wry smile, I have no wish to die that kind of death. When, therefore, the decision was taken to march against the British at Cape Coast I realised that my only chance was either to die a hero's death in battle or to desert to the enemy and be taken prisoner. It is impossible for me to return to Ashanti; I do not know where I can go after I am released but I place myself under the mercy and will of the king of England."

They had listened fascinated and engrossed to Kwabena Opoku's vivid story not only because the old clichés about fighting a bunch of savages and uncivilised blacks were simply not true but also because the account that the Ashanti warrior had given impressed them by his candour and his sincerity,by the way in which he had expressed his love for this woman and by the shrewd manner by which he had emerged from his dilemma. After some minutes of thought-ful silence the commanding officer said.

"Horrocks, we've taken this enemy officer prisoner but I think that as he has saved the life of one of His Majesty's officers and as we have both listened to his very succinct and moving story the least that we can do is to give him his release with effect from now. I would go so far as to suggest to you that you might employ him as your personal servant until you return to England and then perhaps you could give him a gratuity for services rendered."

So the matter was arranged. After Kwabena Opoku and the interpreter had withdrawn, the commanding officer remarked, "You might like to know, Horrocks, that we held off the Ashanti right along the line and that they have re-grouped further up the track. They suffered heavy casualties from our rifle fire and they never once got closer than thirty yards."

"What happened to my platoon, Sir?"

"They took the full force of the Ashanti combat troops, they'd gone back further down the track so that they were in a position to assault you on three sides. It had all been carefully worked out. They broke into your square but your chaps fought so gamely with bayonets at close quarters that they couldn't get any further with their flank attack and were beaten back. You lost six men and there are a dozen or so with stab and spear wounds but they and all the others have reported in. Your corporal rallied them, you've trained him well. You have good reason to be proud of what your men achieved. The Major-General is pleased with the way your men held the line long enough for reinforcements to come; you know, for a time, you were outnumbered ten to one. We are sorry that you are out of the war, Horrocks, but you and your men have already played a notable part in it. It will not be forgotten."

Kwabena looked after Henry Horrocks until his thigh wound healed sufficiently for him to be transported back to England. It was then that the British officer put into effect a decision that he had for quite some time been debating in his mind. Kwabena should accompany him to England as his personal servant and should live with him in his home near Wareham in Dorset. Horrocks was a bachelor and he would in future share his life with the man who had saved it. He had come to appreciate the many sterling qualities that Kwabena possessed, he saw in him the merits of the good soldier and officer: personal discipline, orderliness, readiness to serve and to act on his own initiative. Once Kwabena had learned English, and he had already made good progress, he would be a good companion and a great help on the farm. Henry had never married but he had a daughter, Beatrice, who kept house for him as her mother had done until her untimely death some years ago and he had formally adopted her and had made her his heiress. Kwabena like most Africans quickly learned the new language and spoke it with a definite Dorset accent which endeared him to the local people and in course of time he became a well-liked figure in the district. Captain Horrocks had written an account of the Ashanti campaign which had been printed in Dorchester so that everyone knew how Kwabena had saved his life. It was a great day when Kwabena was baptized as a Christian in the Wareham parish church and it was then that the vicar had anglicised his name to Benjamin Berricombe! He had assumed that Ben (as he was called by everybody) was the short form of Benjamin while Berricombe was a village on the south coast. So it was that when in 1890 Beatrice and Ben were married, Berricombe had already become their accepted surname. The three Berricombe children all had the warm, silky-brown skin of half-castes but it didn't seem to matter, many Dorset fishermen were just as swarthy and they grew up as thoroughly integrated English children.

That was how the Berricombe family, with its origin in the Gold Coast became established in Dorset and why a grandson of Kwabena Opoku from Berekum who was born in 1930 and who was christened Reuben became specially interested in that country in West Africa. He had been educated at Sherbourne School and at Exeter University where he had studied Mathematics, Music and Geography with special reference to tropical countries. He possessed an old tattered copy of the small book by Granddad Horrocks about the 1873-74 Ashanti war which he had read avidly many times. It was amazing that both Granddad Horrocks, as he called him, and Granddad Berricombe had fought on opposing sides in that war! The idea that one day he would visit the Gold Coast had grown in his mind. He had trained as a teacher and when the new independent country of Ghana had emerged he offered himself for service there as a teacher in 1958 with the British Voluntary Service Overseas (VSO) organisation. The formalities hadn't taken long and in the July of that year when he landed at Accra Airport he was met by Tom McKenzie who introduced himself as the VSO representative in Ashanti. Tom was about 45 years old, lean, active, friendly and sympathetic and always had a humorous twinkle in his eye and who gave an immediate impression of capability as a man who was thoroughly at home in Africa, as indeed he was, having worked there for the last dozen years. He was a Scot who had been recruited by the Church of Scotland Foreign Mission Committee to the staff of the Presbyterian Training College in Akropong where he had made a great impression. He had learned to speak Twi in record time, a rare achievement among the British; the German and Swiss missionaries were far superior in this respect. Indeed Twi in its Akwapim form had first been reduced to writing by J. G. Christaller in 1859 a feat he followed by his comprehensive dictionary in 1874. Twi or Akan is the parent language, Akwapim, Fanti and Ashanti are forms or dialects of it. If you speak one of the forms you can be understood by more than three-quarters of the people of Ghana. Tom McKenzie also possessed a thorough knowledge of traditional Akan religion and customs and of the way of thinking of the African as well as of the history of the country and of the different tribal groupings. Before independence he had been Manager of Presbyterian Church schools in Ashanti and after independence all the churches with government agreement had appointed him General Manager of all the former mission schools. Naturally there had been intense rivalry among the churches because they had all used the school-planting method as their main evangelistic weapon: every town and village had one or other of these denominational schools for the upkeep of which central government paid grant in the form of support for teachers and it was inevitable that some of this money would be used to support the church. The size of the contribution of the missions to educational provision can be estimated from the fact that in 1958 there were 605,000 children in church primary schools: the Catholics, Presbyterians, Methodists and Anglicans accounting for four-fifths of the total, the remainder belonging to small sectarian groups. Just as in European countries the animosity among the churches had harmed the religious and social unity of the people, in the same way in Ghana Akan traditional social solidarity was affected.

Tom McKenzie had succeeded in winning the confidence

of the different denominations in his efforts to achieve fairness and everyone praised his constant striving for high standards of learning in the schools.

For newcomers into the teaching service in Ghana he was an excellent guide and the Education Department had asked him to take the American Peace Corps and the British VSO expatriates under his wing as well. He planned to start a new secondary school in Bechemantia a small town north of Bechem about 80 km. north-west of Kumasi. At one end of the town there was a large house which was in reasonable repair because it had been used for a time as a rest house. Tom McKenzie thought that it would provide temporary accommodation for some of the teachers, Reuben could go there and he had had recent news of the probable arrival of a Peace Corps woman teacher by name Thelma Morrow from the United States; with five teachers and the two expatriates the new school could make a start.

Tom greeted Reuben warmly at the airport and led him to his Land Rover in the car-park where they added Reuben's suitcase and rucksack to the school materials, supplies and foodstuffs that were already there. It would be good to have someone to talk to on the way north, there was a lot of important information to impart but he would do it in an interesting way and he felt sure that Reuben would be an intelligent listener.

"You can call me Tom, what is your preferred name?"

"I am known by everybody as Ben. You know my Granpa was a native of the Gold Coast, he was called Kwabena Opoku and came from Berekum in northwest Ashanti. That's the real reason why I am here, to learn at first hand something of the world of my African ancestor."

"So you already have a built-in interest in the country and especially in Ashanti? That's a very good recipe for your success as a teacher especially if you can find time to learn to speak the language. What I propose to do as we drive north is to tell you something about working in this country: climate, health tips for Europeans, the missionary and the educational scene; things like that, that will help you in your work. You won't be able to remember everything but it will serve as an introduction. I'll drive over the Akwapim Ridge where the first missionaries settled and then via Koforidua and Bompata to Agogo where we'll stop two nights in the guest quarters of the Basel Mission hospital. Then we'll drive to Kumasi where you'll stay with me for a few days before beginning your work at Bechemantia not far from Berekum. I'm the General Manager of schools in Ashanti but I also look after VSO and Peace Corps volunteers, whenever you encounter a problem get in touch with me at my office in Kumasi. I'm often on trek but there will always be someone to deal with the message."

"Is the climate always the same the year round, like today, for example?"

"Much the same; there's a rainy season from April to October and a dry season from November to March but this is only a rough guide. If the wind blows from the south-west, from the ocean, it can rain at any time of the year but only during the dry season does the harmattan wind blow from the north-east, from the dry interior and then it can be very dry. There's very little range of temperature night and day, most often between 20° and 35° C but it can often feel hotter than that because the humidity is invariably about 80

% so you can perspire doing nothing. Until you get acclima-tised it can be very enervating."

"Why did the West African coast get the reputation of being the 'white man's grave'?"

"Up to the first World War there was no cure for malaria and no defence against infection; the cause of malaria and other fevers wasn't really known. The main thing is to avoid being bitten by flying insects. As you know, in the tropics, a great variety of insects which feed on human and animal blood flourish and for this reason can transmit malaria, yellow fever, typhoid fever, dengue, and other infections; so for whites the most important health rules are to sleep and rest under a mosquito net, to take your prophylactic tablets at the same time every day, to make sure that your drinking water is boiled and filtered and your food properly prepared. I've got a reliable cook-steward for the house where you will be living with a few other teachers, black and white, so you should be well taken care of."

"We're climbing up the winding road now to the Akwapim Ridge," Tom continued, where the Basel mission-aries began their evangelistic work in 1835. Actually, much earlier, in 1788, when the Danes controlled the eastern part of the Gold Coast, a Dr. P. E. Isert, medical doctor botanist and disciple of Rousseau, who entered the service of the Danish Guinea Company in 1783, planned an agricultural and Christian settlement at Akropong among Africans 'unspoiled' by the worst features of European life on the coast. When he first travelled along the Ridge he gained a wonderful impression of the 'noble savage' who, according to the ideas of Rousseau were living a happy life in complete harmony with nature. His book, published later in German and in a number of European countries was widely read and it re-inforced the missionary appeal. In fact, Isert had good monetary support for his so-called Afrikanische Missionsanstalt which he began but unfortunately in 1789 he died suddenly and in 1794 the project was abandoned. I mention that because the Akwapim Ridge was already known in Europe and when in 1827 the Basel Mission sent four men there, hopes were high but death soon intervened and by 1831 all four were in their graves. Another attempt with three men a year later also failed, the sole survivor being a Dane, Andreas Riis, but he alone reached Akropong and built a stone house there. He was called for ever afterwards by the local people Osiadan, (he built a house)."

"Did Riis succeed?"

"Not really. After four years in Akropong there was not a single convert but his pioneering bore fruit. The next attempt of the Basel Mission had the support of six families and three bachelors of second and third generation liberated Christian African slaves from Jamaica, all Moravians, who volunteered to work for at least two years in Akropong while Riis's new European colleagues were carefully chosen: Johann Widmann from Tübingen, Herman Halleur from Mecklenburg and George Thompson, a young man from Liberia who had been brought to Europe and who had been educated at the seminary in Basel. This time they succeeded. Houses, a chapel and a school were built; Widmann worked hard on the language so that by the middle of 1844 the first Twi hymn was sung and the first school was begun with nine boys. The coffee plantation and the vegetable gardens also began to yield."

"Did they make many converts from among the local

people?"

"No. It seemed clear from the beginning that a Christian community could only be built up in the future from among the children in the school. Don't forget that for most of the missionaries they were working in 'darkest Africa', no one ever considered indigenous religions objectively, no one really thought that African social life had a permanent value of its own. Indigenous social and religious conditions were considered to be so depraved that the Mission made no attempt to work within the Akan social framework or to present the Christian message in terms which made contact with African ideas or way of thinking. The aim was to build up separated Christian groups dedicated to following a completely different way of life. All the Missions were the same; Christianity spread by school-planting and after one generation a permanent cleavage within the local community had been effected. Of course, the local people saw great advantages in schooling and in the ancillary enterprises of the Mission like the Trading Factory that opened stores to buy and market the crops grown by the farmers and to sell general goods imported from Europe where the profits went to support the missionary work. Not only that; there were workshops for the training of Africans as carpenters and joiners, blacksmiths and masons, these were the only technical training institutions in the Colony at that time. Cocoa was first grown by the Basel missionaries on their agriculture plot at Akropong in 1858 and the first road along the Ridge was built by them. So, you see, Ben, according to African understanding of the Christian enterprise, to become a Christian meant getting training of some sort, adopting new social customs, acquiring clerical and artisan skills which got you paid jobs with Government, with trading firms or with the Mission as a teacher, but which, at the same time, to a greater or lesser degree set you apart from the traditional community. It was, in fact, the tangible expression of the missionary ideal of the 19th century: Commerce and Christianity went hand in hand to engender civilisation, expressed of course, in Western European terms; Gospel, School, Trade and Spade would begin a social revolution and bring Africa out of darkness into light. So it was widely believed."

"You mean that the price paid for all this progress was the complete under-estimating of traditional life and its religious values?"

"Yes. There were a few missionaries who strove to express the Christian message in Akan terms but they had little influence; the general tendency was to regard African religion as primitive, decadent and corrupting."

"It's something I should like to know more about when I have time. Incidentally, I keep seeing by the roadside signs which read Presbyterian Church or School, is that the same as Basel Mission?"

"Yes. During the First World War a number of the German missionaries working for the Basel Mission were interned and at the request of the Colonial Government the Church of Scotland sent out personnel who took over the responsibility for the educational work and it was then that the Basel Mission accepted the name Presbyterian."

They had time for a short visit to the College campus in Akropong on a sloping, south-facing hillside dominated by the main college building, flanked by a chapel built in local stone with a stained-glass window in which the figures were African. Further at one side was the original century-old Swiss-style large wooden family house where the Mission had begun. About thirty metres and twelve metres wide the house was built of local stone plastered with red laterite earth then white-washed and roofed with wooden shingles. The living rooms were upstairs while the ground floor rooms provided working space and store rooms. The house had wide verandas on all four sides and was sited east-west so that the sun never reached the walls. The front and rear of the house faced on to quadrangles of vegetable and fruit garden with outbuildings. It was a pattern that became standard all over the country wherever the Basel Mission settled. Further west was the cemetery to be seen, now much overgrown but one could make out the names of some of the pioneers who had sacrificed their lives.

As they stood there Tom said: "You might be interested to know that during the period from 1829 to 1914 the deaths of 140 missionaries are recorded, at least one death every year. Of course, since then the health conditions for Europeans steadily improved so that today with regular prophylactics you can stay quite fit."

They resumed their journey via Koforidua, a large market town, then by the main road north to Nkawkaw and Bompata where they began the climb up on to the Kwahu plateau to Agogo where in 1930 the Mission opened a 60-bed hospital, one of the most-esteemed in the country, now enlarged to 150 beds.

"We shall stay three nights there, Ben, to help you to get used to the climate. They'll have room for us in the guest quarters."

They were warmly welcomed and after a shower and a simple evening meal they slept well in the cooler air of the hills. On the following day Tom took a walk into town. Seen from the hill on which the hospital was built, Agogo lay in a large clearing in the forest at a height of about 500 metres. All around were dark-green forested hills in which were the many cocoa farms but he couldn't see them because cocoa trees need shade and the larger forest trees were, for that reason, not cut down. All the cocoa farms are in the hands of families, there are no large plantations owned by foreigners. Each family has its food farm on cleared and burned land where maize, yams, coco-yams, cassava, groundnuts, plantains and bananas are grown and where a variety of fruits: green-skinned oranges, lemons, pawpaws, melons, pumpkins, okros, green and red peppers are grown. In addition there are coconut and oil palms while gourds which provide calabashes and water-pots are cultivated. The only tools used are the cutlass, a long, heavy, curved knife for cutting, slashing and weeding, and the hoe for tilling.

A wide road flanked with wattle-and-daub houses built on a wooden framework and roofed with corrugated iron sheets led into the town; some of the houses and larger buildings, were built with concrete blocks and roofed with asbestos sheets. The dwelling houses all had a large yard or compound around the circumference of which were extra rooms. In the centre of the town there was the post office, the chief's house, the church and school with a playing field, two large European stores which sold all sorts of goods as well as collecting the sacks of cocoa beans for transport to the railhead at Kumasi. A number of smaller stores offered hardware, household utensils, tinned foods, cloths, flour, sugar, rice, condensed milk, tobacco and cigarettes, razor blades, iron pots, matches, hurricane lamps, furniture, clothing and sandals made from old rubber tires. Another store combined the functions of liquor sales and 'pub'; fermented palm wine as well as beer were being drunk with relish in calabashes at a bar.

Further along the road on the left side Ben was caught up in the bustle and flurry of the market. He lingered in front of some of the stalls: a Fulani butcher was busy slicing a half-carcase of an ox into small, choice pieces; the next stall offered goat's meat, live fowls and snails; alongside there was a stall specialising in salt, peppers, herbs and condiments of all kinds; then came dried fish and silver herrings of different sorts; other booths offered small loaves of soft white bread, balls of kenkey, maize cobs, plain and roasted, assorted lengths of sugar-cane, bananas and plantains, green oranges and limes, tomatoes, okros and small onions. Opposite the market was the so-called lorry park where small and large trucks equipped with wooden planks for seats, plied for hire. The drivers of these 'mammy' lorries waited until the lorry was crammed full with people and produce before they set off to a nearby town or further afield to Kumasi, Accra or Tamale in the north. None of them ran to a timetable; what was important was that you had time to buy what you needed and then to get back safely to your village. There was always room, it seemed, you simply slithered further along your plank pressing closer to your neighbour in order to give the newcomer a bit of space into which wide hips and buttocks made their own way. Passengers and their goods in sacks, in baskets, loose yams and plantains, chickens with tethered legs, babies on mothers' backs, all appeared like a blurred mass as the lorry rolled past. Most of the 'mammy' lorries boasted a colourful painted sign above the driver's cab: often the signs had a religious reference: Love thy neighbour; One with God is a Majority; Never say Die; Roll on till Tomorrow, etc.

The lorry park and the market made a colourful and hectic spectacle, everywhere goods and gear were being loaded from heads into trucks and from lorries onto heads. Children of all ages clustered around. A group of four young girls were playing a dancing game clapping their hands in regular time to a certain tune, then every so often one of them would spring into the centre of the ring, twist her agile body about, stamp or shuffle her feet in a defined way and then jump back into her place. A variation was played opposite another girl by which a leg or an arm would be suddenly thrust out which the girl opposite had to anticipate and to imitate. Two men in the shadow of a tree were playing the game of *warri* with great intensity, the wooden frame with its hollow cups lay between them and both in turn were scooping up and doling out the tokens with great flair and gusto. All around people were conversing animatedly, buying or selling, haggling over a price, striking a bargain or just watching. Ben was fascinated by it all, there was an ebullience, an excitement, a vibrant quality and an animation about this African daily scene which attracted him, maybe, he thought, the sunshine and the warmth had something to do with it but much of the attraction also stemmed from the friendliness of the people, the ready smile that went along with the handshake and the general air of cheerfulness.

Ben had arranged to wait for Tom near the chief's house at five, the time set for his presentation to the Agokrohene. This was the normal custom for a stranger who spent more than 48 hours in the town and at a given signal they entered the courtyard and stood waiting. The chief and his elders, the queen mother, the *okyeame* or spokesman and the young boy designated as the 'soul' of the chief were seated in a semi-circle dressed in their colourful ntamas or cover-cloths, worn like the classical Roman toga. The chief sat on his stool, his head encircled by a narrow green silken fillet while his sleek, brown skin set off to great advantage the gold chain around his neck and the gold bracelet on his arm. Behind the chief, on his left hand, sat Nanahemaa, the queen mother, an elderly distin-guished-looking lady who possessed an air of high breeding. She had elegant, slim, beautiful hands and feet, delicate wrists and ankles, small well-shaped ears lying quite flat against her head which crowned a long graceful neck. In a matrilineal society she occupied a uniquely high position, she was not necessarily the chief's mother, she could be his sister, but she was of royal blood and she had chosen him. She alone could openly rebuke him or the elders or the okyeame and at will question petitioners. No chief in Ashanti could rule without the queen mother. She sat on her chair studded with brass-headed nails and Ben thought that he had never seen a woman quite so dignified and yet so modest.

The linguist or spokesman (okyeame) stood on the right of the chief holding his gold-headed staff of office, one was not allowed to address the chief directly, one's message must be spoken to the okyeame who filled the special role of confidential adviser. He transmitted the message to the chief often in more elegant phrasing together with a comment of his own. He could translate from other local languages and the chief would reply through him.

Tom and Ben shook hands with the group moving from the left of the chief to his right offering the open palm, they were then offered chairs and Tom was invited to speak. A set formula must always be followed which Tom had learned to use: first you asked.

"Is the spokesman there?"

To which the okyeame would reply:

"He is present."

You then requested him as follows:

"Let the chief be informed that we have not come about anything bad but rather to greet him and his elders and to give him certain information."

Tom waited a moment until he received a sign to continue and then said, "Nana knows that I am responsible for the organisation of all the schools in Ashanti and it is now my duty to introduce to him a fresh young teacher from *Aburokyiri* (Europe) who arrived yesterday and who slept last night for the first time in Ashanti."

This information was duly transmitted, to which the chief replied:

"Do you intend to leave this teacher with us in Agokro?"

"Please inform Nana that that there is a special reason why I am unable to do that. The name of the young man is Ben Berricombe and his grandfather was Kwabena Opoku,the nephew of the Berekumhene.

"During the Sagrenti War, Kwabena Opoku was taken prisoner. He led the attack of the combat troops of the Nifahene against the left flank of the British. He was taken to England where he married and had children and where he died in 1918. Now his grandson Ben has come back to Ashanti to teach in a school near Berekum and to find out something about his grandfather's family."

At this information every ear was cocked and every eye was fixed on Ben who had come back from the ancestors this was news indeed! How would the Agokrohene react?

After a short pause the chief beckoned the spokesman over and spoke in his ear whereupon the okyeame announced.

"Because of the importance of this news from Owura McKenzie the visit of Owura Ben from Berekum who has come from Europe back to his own people, we shall hold this evening a special reception for him. There will be drumming and dancing and Ben can speak a greeting to us. Does Ben speak our language?"

"Not yet, but he has the firm intention to learn it. I regret that I cannot leave him with you but I will place him in a new secondary school, in Brong Ahafo. I am sure that Nana will understand the reason for my decision." Tom replied.

"I understand your reason but I hope that this young teacher will find an occasion to visit us again."

The Agokrohene rose, the signal for everyone to stand; Tom and Ben bowed and left the room.

Later that day, in the evening after the sun had set, but not yet dark, they assembled in a large open place behind the chief's house where the crowd of spectators had already formed a large circle in the middle of which the dancing would take place. The ntumpane drums were sounding out different rhythms and staccato phrases, horns were being sounded while the xylophone was playing its accompaniment. This time they sat on the right of the chief who at a given moment gave a signal for the dancing to begin. A women's society wearing identical-patterned wrap-around skirts and blouses performed a set-piece first: they stood in a circle facing inwards, clapping their hands in time to a single drum, then in turn, one after the other moved into the centre of the ring to perform their own solo steps, shuffling and stamping the feet and swinging and swaying the body while the other women sang a kind of chorus hammered out by the xylophone. After that, three or four drums started up, a signal for spectators to join in and soon the entire area was filled with voluptuously-swaying bodies. Sometimes the dancers bent their bodies in a curve close to the ground then rose up with arms flung wide, like swallows in swooping flight, their teeth gleaming white and their dark eyes shining in the light of the moon as their heads rose up. A variant in the dance began, a white piece of cloth started to circulate: any man who had the cloth could throw it onto the lap of a woman or over her shoulders she was then obliged to come out and dance opposite him. She then also had the chance, to choose a partner. Ben and Tom were twice on the dance floor and were able to caper quite creditably.

Then suddenly the floor miraculously cleared, the queen-mother with one of her attendants were performing a graceful and dignified dance together and as they returned to their seats to enthusiastic applause, the chief, followed by his young 'soul' holding up his heavy silk ntama from the rear, stepped into the circle for his long-awaited solo dance. This was the high point of the entire occasion: the chief embodied the deepest feelings, the heartfelt hopes and aspirations, the very existence even of his clansmen and women; he was their vital bond with ancestors, and when they saw that he was smiling, the joy of the crowd knew no bounds. They clapped, called out words of praise: Nana, Agyemang, Osagyefo, Otumfour, the drummers accelerated their tempo until the whole area reverberated with a deafening yet exhilarating sound like the majestic roar of a huge waterfall. After he had danced a few short but skilful steps he held up his right arm and abruptly there was a palpable silence during which he strode a few steps to where Ben was sitting, motioned him to stand up, put his right hand on Ben's head and cried out, "*Oburoni Ababio Akwaaba!*" (White man who has returned, welcome!)

He then embraced him and, followed by his faithful 'soul', returned to his seat. The applause broke out again in a deafening roar; Ben Berricombe from Dorset England had been royally welcomed in Ashanti the home of his ancestor. About two in the morning a select group of elders escorted Tom and Ben back to their quarters at the hospital but the drumming and the dancing was kept up until much later.

Next day as they were driving down the scarp to join the road to Kumasi, Tom said.

"How do you feel after last night, Ben? I hope that you didn't mind my telling them that you had an Ashanti grand-father?"

"No. I didn't mind at all, I was rather flattered in fact to be made such a fuss of, it was so unexpected and personal. I realise that I have a lot to learn about Ashanti ideas and customs."

"You see, Ben, they relish pieces of information like that and it will bring you much goodwill. You have been honoured by the name Ababio, which means 'he has returned'. When a child is born the mother waits with it indoors for eight days when it is brought outdoors for the name-giving and if the baby bears a distinct resemblance to a deceased ancestor it gets the name Ababio as well as its other names. In your case you possess the character and disposition of your grandfather. But it means more than that to the people, it means that you have been sent by the ancestors for a reason; it's not by chance that you're here and they will ask why have you been sent. The obvious reason is that the school in Bechemantia needs teachers and you will be one of them, but these teachers, especially you, will bring exceptional gifts because as Kwabena Opoku's grandson you have skills and abilities from Europe. They will expect much from you for that reason alone, they will link you with their ancestors and be proud to do so. Don't ever forget that, you are one of them now!

"Not that you will be considered as a holy man or anything like that but you will be valued because you have been sent by the ancestors back to the tribe so to speak. Africans are always conscious of their forebears: when they drink, the last drops are poured out on the ground as an act of reverence to them, when they clear a plot in the forest for a farm and feel compelled to fell an old established tree which their forefathers knew, they will pray and pour a libation or make a sacrifice to make sure of the goodwill of the immediate ancestors!

"Now, Ben, as you have become a special person may I give you a few tips to put into action right away: Use your right hand always for giving and receiving anything; point at anything with the right forefinger - the left hand is reserved for dealing with dirty or unclean things. Shake hands always with the open palm, not approaching with the back of the hand; Africans bring gifts when they are invited somewhere or when they are grateful for a service rendered so you should do the same. Learn a few Twi words and phrases as soon as you can so that you can say 'thank you' and exchange greetings when you meet people."

"I've a lot to learn in short time, Tom. How do I start learning the language?"

"One of my colleagues in the office in Kumasi will know

which of the teachers in Bechemantia can best help you. When I was learning I sat in the classrooms of the infant school; that way you hear and imitate the right intonation from the beginning and you can easily follow the text in the reading books they use. It's a phonetic script so once you know the letters and sounds you can read it aloud correctly. I can lend you a few books about Akan traditional customs and beliefs, just read them slowly, don't try to absorb too much at once."

They drove in silence for the most part after that down the scarp, then through dense forest through which the road wound until they reached Ejisu and finally Kumasi the second largest city of Ghana. The cocoa boom had brought Ashanti into the world commodity market and had been responsible for the network of roads along which the tons of cocoa beans were brought by lorry to Kumasi and thence by rail to Takoradi for shipment to the wider world. During the cocoa-growing season much money flowed because from the Cocoa Marketing Board the farmers received a cash advance on half the estimated crop, then at harvest came the final payment based on the actual tonnage produced. As all the farms were owned by private families this money accrued directly to the people who grew the crop. The part played by the large European trading companies like the Union Trading Company from Basel, the United Africa Company from Britain, and the Compagnie Francaise de l'Afrique Occidentale lay in the transport and shipping of the crop and in paying out the cash from the Marketing Board as agents of the Government.

They drove past the huge open market where you could buy every kind of foodstuff as well as an ever-expanding assortment of goods, African and European. The rise in the standard of living was to be seen in the houses of brick and cement, bungalows, apartment blocks, hotels, banks, offices and public buildings. Then along by the railway station thronged by passengers and up the hill by the Mampong road where Tom's house and office were located about a mile from the centre of town. Here Ben stayed in the guest quarters for few days before being taken to Bechemantia.

You might have described Ben Berricombe as typically English in appearance although that is hard to define, he was fresh-faced, rosy-cheeked, his dark-brown hair lay thick and curly on his scalp and there was a friendly openness in his facial expression and in his ready smile. You felt instinctively that he was trustworthy but at the same time he gave out a certain naïve air, as if to say, I am puzzled by a lot of things that I have seen and experienced but I am tolerant, open-minded, and prepared to be convinced. He was above average height, held himself erect, hands often in pockets but all the same he projected an air of eagerness, to help, a readiness to be involved. At school and at university he had played hockey and had run with the cross-country team; he looked fit and was fit. Ben had come so far in his life without any firm commitment to a woman, a certain shyness and diffidence had had something to do with that but study and sport had taken up much of his time and in fact the right girl for him had never appeared. He had, on one occasion, been seduced by a female medical student who had detected in him the qualities that would make a reliable partner, she had invited him to her flat and in exasperation at his failure to take the initiative had taken off all her clothes and had led him into the bedroom. What had happened had not particularly heightened his sexual appetite, she just hadn't been the 'right

girl', that was all. Now, here in Ghana, in a completely different environment, his mind was occupied with assessing the
new experiences that had crowded in during the last few days.

There were doubts and uncertainties. What would it be
like teaching Africans? He knew so little of their background
and of their abilities and had very little time to look into the
textbooks that they were using. At university he had
specialised in Maths and Music but he had been told that
every teacher whose mother-tongue was English would have
to teach that language and as he had an 'A' Level in English
he would have to teach that subject too. Then there had been
that Ababio business at Agogo, had his 'soul' really come
back to earth from the ancestors to play a certain role among
these people? He'd never given much thought to religion, his
parents weren't religious and they had no particular church
affiliation. He had attended church on certain occasions and
there had been some lessons in school on religion but he
really had no clear idea what religious belief was about or
what part it played in human life. Of course, the Christian
religion had formed the character and habits of his people:
there were churches everywhere but not many people
seemed to attend the services except perhaps at times like
Christmas and Easter. Some folk took their children to be
baptized and got married there and when you died a priest or
minister conducted a burial service. But Ben had never
understood the detail of what took place at church services,
like the bread and wine and the things that were sung about
or prayed about which seemed to him highly complicated.
He could appreciate the life and character of Jesus and his
teaching about loving your neighbour but it seemed that you
couldn't just be a follower of Jesus' example, you had to

believe other startling things about his birth and death, and in addition to that there were all sorts of ideas like Holy Spirit, grace, sin, prayer, heaven and hell, which were difficult to define and which didn't seem to have much relevance to normal daily life. What he had learned about Ashanti religion so far seemed to make more practical sense: religion was for everybody, not just for those who happened to believe, everybody was religious in the sense that they belonged to a community on earth that had indissoluble ties with the invisible world where the ancestors dwelt; the world of the spirit and the world of human beings belonged closely to each other. Once his teaching began in Bechemantia he would have a lot to learn. But it felt good to be in a country where he felt at once at home, because of his grandfather he had been given a special welcome and it was now a challenge to him to justify that welcome.

Chapter 3

Akua Bonsu,
Abenaa Francis Macdonald
and Alastair Campbell Anderson

"Such a marriage (*mpena awadie* – the mating of lovers)...
consisted in the open and permanent living together of a
man and a woman without the payment of *aseda* (the so-
called bride price). The children of such a union are legit-
imate and have equal rights of succession with those born
from strictly regular unions".

R.S.Rattray, *Ashanti Law and Constitution*, Oxford University Press 1956,
p.30.

In a forest village south of Sunyani on a cold January
morning in the year 1940 a young woman called Akua
Bonsu lay on a mattress suckling her baby Abenaa who
had been born at sunrise.

Four elderly women, the traditional midwives of the
village, had been in attendance on her in the circular swish
and wattle hut reserved for the purpose and during labour
had taken up their accustomed positions around her; the

umbilical cord had been cut, the infant had been washed in water that had not been boiled and had been given to the mother and all four had repeated the traditional Ashanti phrase, "*Asiamasi aba a, tenase*", (As so-and-so has arrived, let her stay). The after-birth had been thrown away on the kitchen midden and the four had departed well satisfied with their night's work and their payment. Because it was a Tuesday, they had been the first to use the baby's natal-day name, Abenaa. The mother Akua was deeply satisfied too, the birth had been relatively easy and the infant was fully formed and healthy. She had scrupulously fulfilled the taboos of her own clan but because Abenaa's father was an officer in the British army and was now with his regiment in Scotland she had invented the rites of her husband's *ntoro* (clan) and had duly performed them before the birth. Before he had been posted back to Scotland he had presented her with a woollen blanket woven with the tartan of Clan Macdonald together with a photograph of himself in uniform on the back of which was written; 'Lieutenant Jaimie Francis Macdonald, his home address and his signature'. So each night during the last month of her pregnancy Akua had solemnly wrapped the blanket around her while uttering the full name of her absent lover and when Abenaa had entered the world she had swaddled her infant in it. Of course, Akua knew that illegitimacy in the sense that the word was used by white people had no significance in Ashanti; the child would be fully accepted into her family and, in any case, in a matrilineal society it was vital to know your mother because she transmits the blood and you inherit through her. In Ashanti the mating of lovers (*mpena awadie*) was fully accepted and recognised; but it pleased Akua that when eight days had passed and the child would be officially presented in public she would have the tartan blanket of her husband's ntoro to show together with the name Francis Macdonald which Abenaa would now bear. No Ashanti could or would possibly object to that. On the contrary, she could prove that the so-called 'bride price', the money which passes between the two families, had also been paid. When Akua had told her lover that she was pregnant he had informed his Commanding Officer who had asked him to follow the standard army procedure, to give her twenty pounds for the confinement and thereafter, at the end of every month, to send her a postal order for two pounds to Kumasi Post Office. He had opened an account for her and she had kept the book carefully hidden away. In fact, all her friends considered Akua to be a lucky woman to have had such a lover and to have borne such a bonny baby.

Akua had met Francis by chance in the Basel Mission bookshop where she was then working and he had enquired about a beginner's book in the Ashanti Twi language. Her English was quite good and thay had talked together and during subsequent meetings she had shown him around Kumasi and had explained to him something of Ashanti history and in turn he had told her of his home in the town of Portree on the island of Skye. After seconday school he had studied at army colleges in Scotland and England and had served in North Africa and Italy during the war before his posting to Ghana. He was 35 years old and had a wife and a young son. Then shortly before his regiment was trans-ferred to Scotland she had given him the news of her pregnancy and he had promised to keep up the payments and had begged her to write to him regularly and to send him photos of the child. She had been proud but deeply sorry to have to say farewell to him.

So now eight days after the birth the traditional naming and outdooring ceremony took place in the courtyard of Akua's family house early in the morning. Relatives and friends were present, libations were poured and prayers were addressed to the ancestors for a blessing on all present and on the child. The baby's first natal-day name, Abenaa, had already been given, the second name should be given by the father, and Akua had already chosen Francis Macdonald so that all the required formalities were complied with. The baby had a warm, light chocolate-coloured skin with grey-blue eyes set in an oval-shaped face topped with curly black hair; it was clear that the father was European. There was nothing unusual in that, in Ghana, children with a white parent were valued; they would be given a European name, sent to school and normally baptised as Christian. Certain European surnames like Baeta, Bannerman, De Graft, Hansen, Hayford, Martinson, Ocansey, Richter, Swanzy, already had a firm place in Ghana history. Abenaa Francis was sent to the local primary and middle schools and later to the Girls' Secondary School in Kumasi. The monthly postal order paid her school fees and when she moved to Kumasi Akua took up her job again as assistant in the Basel Mission bookshop. The puberty ceremony, however, took place on a visit to the village and the event had been celebrated in traditional style. Mother had given the information of Abenaa's first menstruation and on a certain Tuesday forenoon she and her daughter who was dressed in a new ntama and adorned with necklaces and bangles, sat in state under a coloured umbrella at the front of the house to receive the homage of the women of the village who came playing *dono* drums, the only drums that women are allowed to play. A band of young girls, all waving white flags, paraded in front of the house singing *bara* songs which began with congratulations :

Wayo, wayo, ye nua ayo,
Yema no mo, wayade ee!

She has done it, she has done it, our sister has done it,
We say, well done indeed!

Her mother had poured out palm wine from a calabash on the ground with the words: *Nyame, gye nsa nom! Asase Yaa, gye nsa nom! Nsamanfo,*

Munye nsa nom!
Oba yi a Nyame de ama me yi, nne na wabo no bara!

(O God, take this wine and drink! Earth Mother, take this wine and drink! Ancestors, take this wine and drink! For today this girl whom God gave me has become a woman!)

Early that morning, at first light, Abenaa had been taken by a group of women to a nearby forest stream where the hair of her head had been trimmed and her pubic hair had been shaved; she was then immersed in a pool, dried and dressed in a new cover cloth and carried back to her mother. She had left home as a girl and had returned as a woman. When her menstruation was over she had gone round the village in her fine clothes returning thanks to the women who had taken part in the ceremony. Traditionally Abenaa was now in a position to receive an offer of marriage but like most educated girls she had preferred to wait, to follow a career for a time until a suitable man appeared. She and her mother lived in a rented flat in Harper Road and followed an urban life-style wearing European dress during the day and

African dress in the evenings. Abenaa tied her black hair in a pony tail beneath which her oval face showed to advantage: her grey-blue eyes regarded you with sympathetic interest and her lips parted in a ready smile. It was hard to discern from her features which elements were dominant, Ashanti or Scots, so well-blended were they. In traditional Ashanti dress she looked African, in European dress she looked southern European. She was now in the second year of an intensive Business Studies and English Language course at the university, the diploma of which would ensure her a good post in one of the firms or in Government.

Abenaa was in the habit of using the canteen in the afternoons for study, it was often empty at that time and she had more room to spread her books than at home; it was cooler too and she enjoyed the view over the green grass and the hibiscus bushes in flower and beyond them the movement of people and traffic. The Accra bus drew up at the gates and a young white man with ginger hair and a reddish face got out wearily,collected his suitcase and duffelbag from the trailer, then stood undecidedly before walking through the gates and turning into the canteen. He bought a Fanta at the counter and sat down at a nearby table to quench his thirst. He had no doubt been informed that accommodation was available for visitors cheaper than in hotels in town, so Abenaa thought, but why shouldn't she speak with him and ask if he needed advice? The stronger motivation was the chance to talk with a white student about her own age; she knew about her father in Scotland, her mother had spoken about him often enough, now here was the opportunity to get to know a white man newly arrived. She caught his eye, smiled and said in a friendly tone in English.

"Welcome to Kumasi, can I help you?"

"Thank you; yes, I've just arrived off the Accra bus, I flew in from London yesterday. I was told that I could get a room in the university and that there were frequent buses into town."

There was warmth in his deep voice and to her surprise he pronounced his words so clearly that she had no problem at all in understanding him. She moved to a chair opposite him.

"They normally have a number of single rooms to let. How long do you plan to stay?"

He hesitated before replying.

"My uncle and aunt are somewhere in Ghana but I don't know exactly where."

"Perhaps I can help you to find them?"

"It's not urgent, it's just that...." Again he was uncertain what to say, how could he confide in a stranger whom he had met only five minutes ago? Yet there was a manifest sincerity in the manner of this Ghanaian girl and he had such an urge to talk to someone about his utter failure at university and his sudden decision to come to Ghana that he asked her.

"Can you spare an hour to listen to my miserable tale? I've given up my studies at a university in England. No, that's not true, I was expelled because I was lazy and failed my exams ... and I suddenly thought that I would fly to Ghana to talk with my aunt and uncle."

"Why didn't you go home?"

"I was ashamed because my parents had great expectations of me, so I had this vague idea, maybe I could continue my studies in Ghana and make a career there."

He seemed anxious to talk and Abenaa fetched two cups of coffee and sandwiches from the canteen counter.

"What were you studying in England?"

"Agriculture: farming, crops, animal husbandry, the economics of farming, that sort of thing."

"Is your father a farmer?"

"Yes. He rears sheep and cattle, grows oats and potatoes and on the estate there is woodland and hill pasture so he wanted me to study agriculture so that I could bring in new ideas and methods."

"Wasn't that a good idea? It's mainly cocoa farming in this country and to take over a family farm would be considered a good thing."

"I suppose so, but the prospect didn't really attract me and at university I got involved in radical left-wing political protest groups that took up most of my time."

"What were you protesting about?"

"Well, I suppose we felt that the entire social system in Britain was unjust. Most of us were communist-inspired and we wanted to change everything that we had inherited from the past or abolish it, like aristocracy, capitalism and big business, colonialism and all kinds of expoitation and privilege. The were also many 'green' students who protested against the destruction of forests, the use of atomic energy, research in poison gases, and the destruction of the environment by car exhausts and by toxic waste in rivers and seas. Most of us felt that change could only come by aggressive action like sit–ins, picketing, blocking roads and occupying public buildings so as to force the authorities to change their policy. There were always large demonstrations somewhere or other which we joined in and often clashes with the police. So you see, there wasn't much time left for study. Some of us felt guilty if we came from wealthy or traditional landed families: you see, my father belongs to the Campbell clan, he is the local laird , a sort of sub-chief and although he is not rich, he occupies a privileged position."

"In Ghana we have always had chiefs and sub-chiefs but they are elected by the people who can always de-stool them."

"De-stool ? What does that mean?"

"It means that they can force him to resign for mis-use of public money or for offences against traditional laws and customs. Our Prime Minister has taken away some of their powers in his aim to build up a more socialist-African type of community. Our people too, realise that social change must come but at the moment their main interest is in the basics like electric light, piped water, tarred roads, more hospitals and schools, and good communications, and I think that our students are much too conscious of their privileged position to spend time on the kind of protests that you mention. They just want to study and train for something that will be useful and profitable in the modern world. Maybe later we might think about changing the traditional social system which has served us quite well for centuries. Do you really think that in Europe you can simply put the clock back and return to a way of life without the knowledge of nuclear fission, or genetics or biochemistry or electronics for example? Maybe the scientists are pressing on ahead too fast but you can't stop them. Think of our situation in Africa compared with yours: your homes are comfortable and full of labour-saving gadgets; you have electric light, piped drinkable water and telephones; your towns have tarred roads, hospitals, schools and a good social system that really functions. When we have what you've got maybe then we'll start being discontented!"

They both laughed. It seemed so absurd when you thought about it like that! It was the first time for ages that he'd really laughed, thought Alastair. He was really tempted to tell her how he had become disillusioned with the student protest obsession and with all their facile theorising about society. His mind was suddenly flooded with memories of the many uncomfortable, disagreeable wasted days spent on sit-ins against fox-hunting, picketing and blocking access roads to government research laboratories, trying to prevent the transport of nuclear waste, fighting battles with the police, on the university campus wilfully defacing buildings and damaging library books that expressed a traditional or conventional point of view, while certain professors who were on the hit-list found their studies vandalized. And afterwards they had gloated over their exploits; in one case when they had laid invisible obstacles for fox hunters and had caused a teenage girl to fall heavily and to break a collarbone; each new episode in the Greenpeace saga was celebrated with delight. Of course, he had met a few serious types but there were many hangers-on, to be gay or lesbian was 'in', while the pill made for easy sex. He'd become fond of a German student from Leipzig called Beate who laughed at his middle class mores and his talk of love, she'd shared her favours with two other males in the sit-in team. Whatever drug was popular they all partook of it and finally he too had succumbed to the habit.

So it was that early one morning he had woken up on a mattress stinking of vomit and urine with a violent headache, an intense feeling of nausea and a strong urge to empty his bladder. He half recognised the room as belonging to one of his 'pals': there was a mixed smell of cigarette smoke, the acrid reek of hashish, spilt beer and his own urine. He had crept to a sitting position but his vision swivelled repeatedly to one side and he waited until the dizziness stopped, then with the help of a chair he had stood up and had made his slow way to the corridor where the toilet was. The stricken face of a stranger looked back at him out of the cracked mirror, a face with sunken, glazed eyes, grey-white skin emphasising two, or was it three days' beard, drooping mouth like that of an old man, even the skin of his neck had begun to hang loose. His hands were trembling but he managed to drag his shirt off – yes, there they were on his left forearm, the tell-tale injection punctures. He had laved water over his face and had gone back to the bedroom where he sank down on the mattress again with his head in his hands overcome by an overwhelming feeling of revulsion, remorse, self-pity and shame followed by a deep sensation of anger at his so-called mates and especially at Beate who had left him alone in his drugged state. It was clear to him now how he had secretly resented their perverse hatred of the so-called 'upper class' of whom he was one; how they had borrowed money from him without any intention of repaying it; how Beate had scorned his tentative words of love; how his own innate tolerance and his need of friends had proved stronger than his disgust at some of the things they said and did. How utterly boring their mindless jargon that they spouted by heart like cartoon robots had become to him! Beate was a prime example: she always kept a dead-pan expression and when she spoke, it was like listening to a tape-recording of Marxist theory. One of her favourite themes was that it was justifiable to use violent means of protest because the police are the agents of oppression. You couldn't interrupt her rigmarole once she got started. It was also clear to him now that she had seduced him just to show how emancipated she was, she had been truly programmed with communist stereotyped political and social jargon!

He had searched for his jeans; yes, sure enough, the banknotes in his wallet had gone, he struggled to get dressed somehow and before he left he tore down the posters of Fidel Castro, Che Guevara, Sekou Toure, and Patrice Lumumba that had been pasted to the walls. Some of the wallpaper came away as well and he ripped across the self-satisfied faces so that they could not be used again. He had walked slowly back to his lodgings to find on the mat behind the door an official letter from the Vice Chancellor terminating his membership of the university for failing to report for his second re-sit examination. He was literally down and out! He sat at his table with the letter in front of him and wept until finally the germ of an idea came to him, he would go to Ghana and talk with Aunt Ruth and Uncle Neil. He could talk with them much more freely than with his own parents; they would listen without criticising and would advise him. Uncle Neil was in West Africa for his paper covering the post-independence situation in Nigeria and the Congo. He felt that he couldn't possibly face his parents but he would write and tell them where he was. He had looked at his bank book and made a phone call: yes, there was enough money left to buy a air-line ticket to Ghana.

He came out of his reverie; here he was talking to this attractive Ghanaian girl and he didn't even know her name,

"My name is Alastair Campbell Anderson, what's yours?" He asked.

"I'm called Abenaa Francis Macdonald," she replied.

That surprised him.

"How did you come by a Scottish name? Where does the Macdonald come from?"

"It comes from my father, he was a captain in the Black Watch Regiment in the British Army, Macdonald is his clan."

Abenaa spoke proudly, especially to this young man whose appearance and modest bearing had begun to attract her. She smiled and explained.

"I am Scots from my father and Ghanaian from my mother, so you see that I can think and behave like an African as well as like a European."

"Which is dominant? Or are both sides of your personality equal?"

"It depends on where I happen to be or what I happen to be doing. When I am in an African situation I can easily relate to it, in Ghana that is most of the time. When I am learning and reading books in English I can identify with the European or the American standpoint without difficulty, it's often a question of language. But whenever I am thinking about myself the two sides of my personality merge, I'm only one person." She gave him a disarming smile.

Alastair was fascinated by her frankness and sincerity as well as by her command of the English language and felt ashamed of himself for the way in which he had played the role of rebellious student and had not had the guts to be honest with himself. One day, he thought, if their acquaintance continued, and he began to hope that it would, he would tell her all about the shambles of his student days and the time and the money he had squandered.

"I am Scots too, and my father, too, was an officer in the Seaforth Highlander Regiment during the last war."

Suddenly Abenaa had the feeling that her meeting with

this white man was more than coincidence, that there was an element of fate or destiny about it; the Twi proverb *Krabea wonkwati*, (Fate cannot be avoided) crossed her mind, and she abruptly said.

"Listen, stay here on the university campus for the next few days. I want to tell my mother about you, I think she may be able to find lodgings for you near us in Kumasi. The university, in any case, is on vacation from this week-end, and there would be no point in your staying here alone. That will give you time to decide what you want to do. Meet me here tomorrow at 4 in the afternoon, until then relax and sleep, you look tired after your long journey."

Alastair was more than grateful, there was a matter-of-fact, competent, sympathetic air about her that immediately commended her to him. Her attitude was far more agreeable than the usual know-all, self-opinionated indifference of Beate, so he agreed without hesitation. Could it be that here in Ghana among strangers he might be able to make a fresh start to his life?

It seemed so: when Akua Bonsu, Abenaa's mother heard the news and met and talked with Alastair, she was overjoyed and utterly convinced that his arrival was destined. What could be more appropriate than that her daughter should marry the son of a sub-chief of an important Scottish clan? Was not the coming of Alastair a vital confirmation that her own union with Jaimie Francis had been quite a unique event? Could not she now rightly say that his ancestors had willed Alastair's arrival? Akua enthused about him, tall, strong, kind and sympathetic, how like he was to Francis, courteous, reserved, polite, solicitous for her welfare, self-controlled; a man in authority who treated his subordinates with consideration and above all, had treated her like a queen! That was why she had never taken another man in spite of repeated offers and now Nyame had blessed her beyond measure by sending Alastair! She proudly showed to him the Macdonald tartan shawl, Francis' letters and photograph in uniform and told him how they had corresponded three times a year on their birthdays, first to a post box in Portree, Skye, and afterwards in Glasgow. How he had asked each year for a photograph of Abenaa and how he still sent her a postal order every month. She showed him with great joy her Post Office savings book, almost with veneration: so had this man shown his love for me, so proud was he of his child! Then she wanted to know about the Macdonald and the Campbell clans: how far apart were they in Scotland? What was the Campbell tartan like? Were all the Macdonald and Campbell men warriors? Had he a photograph of his father? Akua's curiosity knew no bounds.

All this time Abenaa kept a low profile, she had had in the past few years a few offers of marriage which on the advice of her mother she had refused. In any case she wanted to finish her studies and to follow a career for a few years. But this situation was different, she hadn't fallen in love with Alastair yet although she felt that she could do so. He possessed many of the qualities that she admired in a man but she had no wish to repeat her mother's experience, she wanted a partnership with a man she could respect and love but so far he had no training or career, he had been dismissed from the university, he did not seem to be in touch with his family, he had come to Ghana on impulse and there was no certainty that he would stay, and above all, there had been no words of love between them. There were many things to be resolved before a firm relationship could be established.

But Akua was shrewd, she knew her daughter well and how her mind worked but as far as she was concerned she had not the shadow of a doubt that the union of Abenaa and Alastair was pre-ordained, so she set about oiling the wheels of destiny. She took Alastair on a visit to her cocoa farms: there were three, and interested him in the crop, the planting, cultivation, harvesting and marketing of the beans. She showed him the accounts for previous years in which a tidy net profit had been made but under better management the gain would be greater. Since the Government had made changes in the function of the Cocoa Marketing Board some farmers had been selling their beans across the border in the Ivory Coast; their main problem was transport. That could be overcome by an enterprising young man with the help of Abenaa after her graduation. In the meantime, say for two years, she felt sure that her friend, Dr.Tom McKenzie could find Alastair a post at the new High School that he was planning to open in Bechemantia; he had already suggested to her that Abenaa might be interested in teaching Maths and English there.

It seemed to Alastair that here was the firm prospect of a fresh start to his life but first he would need to talk to his Aunt Ruth, her husband Neil was in the Congo, before she returned to Britain. They met in Kumasi when he told her the whole story of the mess he had made of his time at the university and was able to introduce her to Abenaa and her mother.

"Are you in love with her?" Ruth asked.

"I can't answer that question with a clear 'yes' or 'no' because the only young women I knew at university were the hard-bitten, left-wing political-protest types like Beate, for them marriage and family were out-dated bourgeois customs. You see, Abenaa is the first young woman who has attracted me by her honesty and openness, her simplicity and lack of pretence, she's not playing a role, she's just being herself, I admire her tremendously for that. If you ask her a question about herself, she doesn't fudge around trying to make an impression on you, you just get the plain truth whether it flatters her or not."

"Is she in love with you?"

"We have never spoken together on the subject. Her mother would be delighted if Abenaa fell in love with me but it's much too early to speculate."

"But if you knew that she was in love with you how would you react?"

"I would consider myself to be a very lucky man."

"Would you then consider staying in Ghana, making a career here and asking Abenaa to marry you?"

"Yes, I would."

"That's good enough, Alastair. What Abenaa needs is a clear indication from you over a period of time that you are able to organise your own life successfully from now on. There are the cocoa farms and the transport to organise; you can learn a lot looking after the school farm, the school accounts and supplies, and there would be time to learn the language, and to get to know Abenaa. Can I tell your parents that for the next couple of years you are going to be very busy pulling up your socks and that you have met a very fine girl, half Ghanaian, half Scots?"

Alastair nodded gratefully. That was typical of Aunt Ruth: she listened to you attentively without comment, then asked a few searching questions after which she gave you her advice in a few sentences without reproaches or censure. He would write fully to his parents; their disappointment with his dismal failure at university would be lessened with the news that he was determined to make good here in Ghana. Just imagine if, like his father after the end of the war, he turned up at Shipness with a foreign wife!

That was the way things developed. Alastair and Abenaa talked with Tom McKenzie and felt enthusiastic about joining the staff of the new school and that fact, for Abenaa's mother, was decisive. They would be working together and it could not be long before their relationship would deepen in the direction she wished. But Akua had also her personal secret which she had not yet revealed to her daughter, shortly before the arrival of Alastair she had received a registered letter from Francis in Glasgow informing her that his wife had found out about Abenaa. There had been bitter reproaches and his wife would not be appeased; they had legally divorced and he was now living alone in Glasgow. He had his army pension to live on; should he come to Ghana? This was the main reason why she had been completely convinced that Alastair's coming was fated, it had been ordained by Nyame that Abenaa's father would come back to her and that Abenaa would get a mate from the same land! And what Nyame had decided was unchangeable: didn't the proverb say exactly that?

Asem a Onyame adi asie no, oteasefo nnan no.

(When God has decided something no living person can alter it).

So she had replied by return registered airmail that he should come but to give her as much notice as possible so that she could prepare his daughter. Akua was almost overwhelmed by these events, Nyame was indeed moving in a mysterious way to perform his wonders!

Chapter

❧ *Thelma Nancy Morrow* ❧

"The question of what to do with the blacks is one of the
oldest and guiltiest of America's problems."
Alistair Cooke, *America* p.381, BBC London,1973.

Thelma had always felt a special kinship with her great
grandmother Afua especially after she had become
the keeper of Afua's Gold Coast mementoes, the
brass metal spoon, her waist beads and her cover cloth with
the coloured silk stripe which she had brought with her when
she had been sold as a slave. These keepsakes had been left
with Robert's daughter, who had passed them on to her
brother Paul who, in turn, had entrusted them to Thelma.
Thelma also bore the name Nancy which Oma Afua had
always favoured because it was the name of the brig which had
brought Afua and Bob to Richmond in Virginia, and in
addition she had the surname Morrow, anglicised from
Morree, the fishing village on the Fanti coast where Afua had
lived. Thelma had been born and brought up on the family
farm in Lancaster County not far from Landis Valley where

her great-grandmother and her husband Robert had settled among the Mennonites. Her forebears had fully respected the Mennonite way of life in that they had lived modestly, simply following the teaching of Jesus, living in harmony with nature, conserving resources, respecting the environment, in thrift, self-help and love of their neighbours. She had grown up in this kind of wholesome atmosphere: everyone, whether family, friends or paid workers had a positive outlook look on life, she was cherished by her parents as an only child but not spoiled. Her mother and aunt Roberta had often spoken to her about Afua so that the keepsakes that she had became like talismans, it thrilled her to think that she had the same blood and DNA as Afua. At school she had read books about the slave trade that saddened her and made her angry that in her own country the whites had insisted on separate development for the blacks. She identified herself with the struggle of the blacks in the USA and secretly thought how splendid it would be to work in Ghana to experience at first-hand African life.

That was, however, only one side of the story, she wanted to work in Africa to have enough time to sort out her own personal life. She was aware that she generally made a favouable impression on other people, that they saw her as modest, somewhat reticent, sympathetic, well-mannered, intelligent and capable. She dressed plainly, used little make-up, wore few rings or jewellery, her chestnut hair was cut short, she was usually cheerful, easy to talk to and mixed well with people. But, and a big 'but' it was, what no one perceived were her deeply ingrained sexual feelings. Sometime she felt ashamed at the ambivalence within her personality as a result of her experiences with Wayne Baker, her Science teacher and with Duncan Larsen, a fellow student at Johns Hopkins University. Wayne lived a mile away from the farm and he had ferried her and her friend Elsa to school and back. When Elsa left school Thelma had travelled alone with him daily. He was about 60, grey-haired, fresh-faced, active and youthful in manner, a widower with two grown-up children who lived somewhere in the mid-West. He lived alone, kept bees and tended his herbal garden and possessed a mine of information about the medicinal properties which he had researched. He was a highly-respected member of staff and of the community, who after the death of his wife twenty years before had never married again.

Their affair had started,so it had seemed to her, quite casually and almost involuntarily. As he leaned across her to open the car door for her, his hand had rested on the thigh next to him and then he placed a warm hand gently on one breast. She had found the touching quite pleasant, even wished that it could have been prolonged. For some time afterwards nothing further had taken place but for her 18th birthday he had given her a carefully-selected bunch of flowers from his garden, had kissed her on both cheeks and then on the lips and on the following Friday afternoon had invited he into his cottage and had locked her into a tight embrace. She had felt no fear, no anxiety, only a curious, intense anticipation and only after they had lain together did he break the silence.

"For twenty years I have lived without sex. Do you think that you can keep this relationship a secret?"

She replied at once knowing that what had happened had satisfied a deep need for her too.

"Of course, I can. No one must ever get to know."

As she later pondered over the encounter her first emotion was pride; she felt proud that he had chosen her, proud that she could satisfy his physical needs, proud that she could be the confidante of a man so much older and wiser than herself, a man whose tenderness and sympathy affected her deeply. Her second emotion was a deep anxiety: how could she be sure that her family would never get to know? Her parents were no longer members of the Mennonite group but a puritan-type of moral code was strong in her family: you worked hard, you were disciplined and strict in your own life, clean, tidy, frugal, abstemious, absolutely honest, faithful to marital vows, no aberrations like fornication or adultery. If her affair with Wayne were to become known it would bring disgrace on her family which could never be overcome. Yet, from that time on, she worked harder at school than ever before, learning became something which brought them together, they discussed ideas and problems as they travelled to and from school. Wayne never spoke of the future of their relationship and she was intuitively aware that there could be no future – she would go on to university and he would retire and leave the district – but for now their close attachment meant much to them both. Their association was the gateway to the sharing of thoughts and feelings and the difference of age had no significance: his reticence, shyness and sense of isolation disappeared, while for her their intimate association rid her of inhibitions, she felt more at ease with herself, more mature, less tense, how could she express it, more tolerant, more human even.

Then later, at Johns Hopkins University she had met a fellow student, Duncan Larsen, on a class visit to Baltimore.

She had become aware of his appraising glances and they had exchanged smiles so that on the return journey he had taken the seat next to her. She had been flattered to have been picked out for his attention. He was lanky in build, broad-shouldered, narrow-waisted, light-brown, crisp hair above a pair of intelligent blue eyes, good, capable hands, altogether a clean and healthy-looking regular young American. He spoke first.

"Funny that we've never met up before."

"It's rare when you're not in the same faculty."

They had exchanged names, shared information about their courses and their future plans and had made a date for the following week-end. It had been the first of regular wek-end dates when they talked of their respective families, of their likes and dislikes and had found that they had much in common. Both were open and forthright in speaking their minds, each felt a respect for the other and they had become close friends. Their intimacy had increased and shortly before graduation they had spent an afternnon on a deserted Maryland beach, had shed their clothes and had lain together. The had each met the other's family who had tacitly approved of the match and it seemed that all was set fair for a marriage in the near future.

Until Wayne left the district she had kept up her relationship with him and it was at that time that she began to be deeply unsure of herself as though her psyche had played two different roles with two different men. This was the reason why the Peace Corps plan had remained firmly in her mind, to take up a post in Ghana would remove her from the scene, so to speak, and would give her the chance to resolve the ambivalence within her personality. Her motivation to work with the

Peace Corps was genuine enough but it would also give her a breathing-space in which to come terms with herself. At Johns Hopkins University in Baltimore she had majored in European and African History and in Anthropology, trained as a teacher and had taught in a downtown high school in Baltimore. Her letter of enquiry to the Peace Corps Directorate in Washington was given a prompt reply inviting her to a preliminary interview; she was welcomed by the Director, Pauline Jones, who began by asking.

"Do you know where you are? Not far from the Library of Congress and the Supreme Court; quite nearby is the Frederick Douglass Institute of African Art and History. Frederick Douglass was a black slave who died in 1895, his father was white, his mother a black farm worker, and who spent much of his adult life campaigning for the rights of freed slaves. Both Presidents Lincoln and Grant consulted him and during his lifetime he collected many sculptures and works of art from Africa which form the foundation of the present Museum of African Art. What decided you to write to us?"

"The main reason for my decision was that my great-grandmother was brought to the USA as a slave in 1826 and my grandfather was born a year later on a plantation near Richmond, Virginia, his father was the third mate of the ship that brought them over and who came from Boston. My parents used often to talk to me about them and certain keepsakes of Afua – that was her name – the only posses-sions she had when she left Africa, were handed down to me. So you see, I developed a special interest in Ghana and I should like to go and work there."

"That's really interesting, my grandfather was a slave too and that's why I work for the Peace Corps and support the activities of St. Augustine's Church on 15th Street which has become an important centre for blacks. Freed slaves started a school for their children in 1858 and built a chapel nearby, they were encouraged by President Lincoln and once they had raised 1500 dollars they began building the present church which now has become an influential organisation for furthering the interests of black people. The choir is famous for its singing of Gospel Songs and Blues at services, melodies like 'When the saints go marching in', 'Nobody knows the trouble I've seen', 'Shadrach, Meshach and Abednego'. You know, for the blacks, religion, politics and music all belong together; the fight for full civil rights is part of their religious belief."

"Another reason for my decision is to try to probe deeper into the race problem. When you reflect on what we know of human origins it seems clear that our earliest ancestors came out of Africa, Africans have a longer history on earth than any other race, while the variations in skin colour, facial and other physical features represent adaptation to climatic differences during the last million years. Where did the prejudice against blacks come from? Of all the immigrant groups who arrived in the USA the blacks are the only ones who came in chains and who had lost their identity for ever. Are we ever going to assimilate them as equal citizens into our society?" Thelma continued.

"You raise an important issue that I have long puzzled over. I think that much of the prejudice and the discrimination stems from the feeling that whites have of their technical superiority, they give grudging praise to the artistic and organisational abilities of the Ashanti, the Baule, the Yoruba of Benin, to speak only of West Africa, but in fact, during the colonial period European culture and civilisation dominated, there was almost no reference to indigenous ways of thinking and living. Even the Christian Missions downgraded the African expression of religion. There was almost no attempt anywhere to find points of contact between the thought-world of Africans and the Christian scheme, to become a Christian meant abandoning everything African, giving up their traditional religion and way of life and become 'europeanised'. It was an easy step from that point of view to equate black and brown skins with ignorance and backwardness."

"All that I learned about my great-grandmother Afua was that she was a fine person, hard-working, skilled in whatever she did, wise and kind and loving – virtues that Americans so admire – but she had a brown skin and some African facial features, she spoke clear and good English and she could read, write and reckon better than many whites," Thelma said.

"I agree with you entirely. Now let me explain the Peace Corps programme. It's much like the British organisation called Voluntary Service Overseas (VSO) where young qualified persons like yourself volunteer to work for a year or two in schools, hospitals and with social agencies. We ask governments where they need help. We have a teacher in Uganda who has gathered together a group of uncared-for AIDS orphans and has organised them into a self-help commune: they've built huts and classrooms, made some of their own furniture, they are growing some of their own crops and two local teachers are working there. A young man from Philadelphia has joined the staff of the only school for blind children in Ghana; another teacher has joined a team in Botswana working with formerly nomadic Bushmen, but mostly our people are teaching in schools at all levels from kindergarten to secondary. In each country we have a responsible senior person who will help you with accomodation and any other problems but you need to be self-reliant, good-tempered and adaptable, ready to make the best of a difficult situation.We'll pay your travelling costs but we can't provide you with a car, we make an allowance for subsistence and we'll give you a cash allowance equal to the local salary. We'll make sure that you get local leave and we cover all medical expenses. Are you interested so far? When I got your letter I thought that you would fit in very well with a new teaching project in Ghana that we know about."

"Yes, I am still interested."

"In that case, make a formal application on the form, you can be assured that my committee will be most impressed by your qualifications and experience."

Thelma walked away from the interview to the rail station in a thoughtful mood. Along Constitution Avenue there was a black protest group making their appeal in sight of the White House, descendants of slaves uprooted from Africa who wanted to put real roots down as Americans with no discrimination, but in spite of emancipation at the end of the Civil War, almost a hundred years before, they seemed as far away as ever from achieving their aim. After the Proclamation of 1863, thousands of freed slaves had made their way to Washington and now, in a city of over half a million inhabitants, 70% of whom were blacks, they were still denied full rights as citizens under the Constitution: there was still segregation in the schools and separation in housing, some suburbs 'white' and others 'black'; but the notion of equal but separate development had never worked.

Then her own personal problem filled her mind, she felt pretty sure that her formal application would be accepted so the next step would be to put her parents fully in the picture but with Duncan it was not going to be easy. She had never discussed her Peace Corps plan with him but now that she had gone so far she felt obliged to do so. He would be driving over at the weekend and she could introduce the topic then when they were alone.

When he arrived she suggested a hike round the fruit farm.

"I was in Washington last week," she said.

"Doing what? Shopping or visiting?"

"Neither, I was being interviewed for a job with the Peace Corps in Ghana."

"Overseas? I thought that our plan was that you would stay in Baltimore until I was through at M. I. T. and then we would marry. What's this Ghana business all about anyway? Why haven't you ever discussed it with me?"

"I've wanted to go to Ghana for a long time. You know that my great-grandmother was brought from there as a slave; Robert, her son, my grandfather was also a slave although he was born in the U. S. on a plantation near Richmond. His father was a merchant navy officer who hailed from Boston. So I've always had a secret ambition to visit Ghana to search for my roots. But I've always been shy of disussing it with anyone, even with you."

"How long do you plan to be away?"

"The Peace Corps would prefer a two-year contract."

"But you also have roots in Germany, I think. Do you plan to go there too?"

"No. The history of the German Mennonites is well-documented, I know all I want to know about them."

"Why should you feel specially involved with your African roots? Surely it's not all that important? You don't need to tell anyone that you have African ancestors."

As soon as he had said that, Duncan realised that he had blundered when Thelma retorted sharply.

"But why should I ever want to hide the fact? I'm not ashamed that African blood flows in my veins and that I have inherited African genes. What I am ashamed of is that I live in a country where blacks make up 30% of the population but who are everywhere discriminated against. When I studied the slavery question and learned what happened to the slaves after they were sold at auction like cattle, and what has happened to them since emancipation, my wish was strengthened to visit West Africa to get to know them at first hand. For years I've felt personally involved in the one problem that for over three hundred years the US has not been able to solve, what to do with the blacks. It's the oldest and guiltiest of America's problems."

"Look Thelma. You know very well that I was brought up in a family where blacks are regarded as OK as servants and OK for menial work and routine jobs but otherwise not really intelligent or gifted enough to take a full part in our society. That's how the idea of equal but separate developed."

"How can you talk about the intelligence of the blacks when they have never been given an equal place in our educational system? In any case, why should they be kept separate? They're human beings like whites, same genetic structure, same physical and mental equipment, all *homo sapiens*. The outward differences are literally only skin-deep;

why should the blacks be singled out for this treatment and not the Chinese, the Japanese, the Hispanics, our own Indians? Doesn't our national motto, *e pluribus unum* mean just that, a multi-racial society? What's special about a white or a pink skin? Of all the human beings world-wide, whites are in a distinct minority and it seems to be moving that way in the US."

"All that may be true for you, Thelma, but I just can't see it that way. My family and millions of whites in the USA would never accept a situation where blacks held political control. You see the reaction to the agitation for the integration of black and white kids in schools, they are dead against this civil rights stuff and confrontation."

"Well, the way I see it is that we are wasting a lot of time and money resisting something that in course of time is going to happen anyway. What do you plan to do when blacks and the other minorities are in a majority?"

"That's a long time off and as of now I'm not particularly bothered about it, the politicians are paid to deal with these matters. I don't pretend to have an answer to these questions; what bothers me right now is the personal thing between us. You say that you will be away in Ghana for the next two years and I'm not at all sure that I could accept waiting that long; in fact, I had thought that we could be in a position to marry fairly soon, I mean, before I was through with my thesis. I know that my parents would help us financially and once I was through college and in a job we could start raising a family."

For Thelma this gave a different perspective to the discussion and it was another topic that they had never touched on, namely, her career. She knew instinctively that Duncan would make her a good husband but it was clear that her own career would take second place to his and in due course making a home for her husband and children would soon become the most important activity of her life. That, at this stage, she didn't want; she wanted to continue teaching, she wanted to work in Ghana, she wanted time overseas in a completely different environment to sort herself out.

"So you would prefer me to give up my plan for Ghana to fit in with your notion of an early marriage? And along with that, if I understand you right you would prefer me to give up my special interest and concern with the racial question and to keep quiet about my African ancestry?"

Duncan hesitated, they had reached a crucial point and he was quite clear that there would be no going back on the reply that in all honesty he had to give.

"Yes, I think I do. Why concern youself with such political and racial questions ? Is it so important to you to seek out your roots in Ghana? Why, for God's sake? Why can't we just get on with our own lives?"

"Don't you understand, Duncan? I just couldn't put these matters on one side, I couldn't hide my African heritage away as though it hadn't happened or as if it had no significance. My family would find it very odd that I never spoke about Oma Afua any more. If my great-grandmother hadn't been brought to America as as slave I wouldn't have been born. Don't you see? The colour and racial questions are literally in my blood, a fundamental part of me, it would become more and more difficult for the two of us to stay together unless you changed your views."

Duncan once again hesitated but he had to be honest with Thelma and with himself.

"I don't think that I could do that, Thelma, I guess that I

would go along with the attitudes of my family."

"Then it looks as if we should say goodbye, Duncan, for keeps. I simply have to go through with my plan to work with the Peace Corps in Ghana and I just can't ever forget my African heritage."

They both instinctively realised from all that had been said that their love affair under these new circumstances could go no further. Duncan was surprised at the strength of Thelma's convictions and he admired her for it while Thelma blamed herself for not having spoken on this topic to Duncan earlier. He took both of her hands in his, looked into her eyes.

"I always thought that we had something very special going for us, we have had some great times together and we have a lot in common but I guess you are right Thelma, this Africa thing of yours would have proved too difficult for us to overcome."

She suddenly felt the distressing pain of final parting but there was no turning back from her decision, she could only blurt out,

"Dear, dear Duncan, I shall miss you a lot and always think of you."

She freed her hands, quickly turned and walked away without looking back. She heard his car drive away and in her room threw herself onto the bed and wept bitterly.

A week later, as she returned to her Baltimore flat, a letter from Pauline Jones awaited her appointing her as a teacher of African History and English Language at the new Bechemantia High School in Ashanti, Ghana subject to a medical examination. Her Peace Corps supervisor would be a Scotsman called Dr. Thomas McKenzie who would meet

her at Accra Airport and make all the residential arrangements for her. There was a thick package of informative
brochures which would take her days to absorb; her tourist
class flight by PanAm had been reserved for October 20th so
that she had just a month to prepare. It all sounded exciting
and reassuring and she checked in the atlas just where she
would be working. One thing was clear she would be a
longish way from the Fanti coast where Afua had lived as a
girl but not so far from Bekwai where she had been taken as
a prisoner after the battle of Asamankow in 1824. She felt
very pleased at the way things had worked out, now she had
much to think about and to make ready.

In fact, in retrospect, it hadn't seemed long at all before
she was stepping out of the huge PanAm Boeing into the
bright sunlight and the humid warmth of a typical Ghana
day, she identified her luggage and was greeted by the
passport officer with the word *akwaaba* (welcome) and at the
exit gate stood a tall, lean figure in a khaki shirt and slacks
holding aloft a white card with her name on it. When he
caught her gaze he smiled broadly and raised his felt bush hat
to her, she felt the warm clasp of his hand as he greeted her.
Dr McKenzie seemed to be in the mid-forties in age and had
a capable air about him. He called to the porter who held the
trolley to follow them to the car park and to stow the cases
in the Land Rover.

"Pauline Jones sends her warmest greetings," she said.

He was clearly pleased.

"I've met her only once when she made a tour of West
Africa and I was able to show her something of Ghana and we
had the chance to exchange information on Peace Corps and
VSO and I was able to put her in the picture about schools in

this country. We've corresponded since then and when I told her of my plan for a new secondary school in Ashanti she said she would look out for someone and recently wrote to me about you; I was delighted. We're on our way now to the University at Legon where you will stay overnight with friends of mine, the Fosters, Jim and his wife both worked for some years in the USA so you will not be short of conversation topics. I have business in Accra but I shall pick you up after breakfast tomorrow for the drive to Kumasi."

In fact Tom – everyone called him that – arrived early and they all took breakfast together before setting out. He seemed eager to talk and Thelma was happy to listen.

"I've booked a nice room for you in the Basel Mission Guest House in Kumasi, it's in the middle of the town so that you can easily walk around, then as soon as the house in Bechemantia is ready, I reckon in about two weeks, you can move up there. You've really arrived in nice time because the plan is to open the school in January and there is still a lot to do. I suggest that during the drive to Kumasi you ask me as many questions as you like about the school because I really would appreciate your views and comments especially with your American high school experience."

"What intrigues me most is what inspired you to want to found a new school?"

"It was the example of the middle school system set up by the Basel missionaries: already by 1870 the pattern was simple, six years in primary school followed by four years in the middle school, the pupils' ages were roughly 13 to 18, like your high schools. The middle schools were both boarding and day. All the normal subjects, including crafts, singing, gardening, bookbinding, masonry, woodcarving and modelling were well-taught by well-motivated teachers including missionaries. The Christian element was strong and discipline was strict as you would expect, but the rewards were considerable: the pupils got good jobs afterwards in Government service, with the trading firms or they became catechists and teachers in the Mission's schools, they were the elite of their time. I was attracted by the all-round character of the schools."

"You mean that your new high school would fill a similar role? Isn't elite kind of out-dated in these egalitarian days?"

"Yes. I should have used the word 'excellence' to describe the aim of the school. A school is a place where learning takes place in every subject and a school's staff should be flexible enough to ensure that every pupil benefits, there should be no failures – every child is good at something and it's the task of the staff to find out what it is. Not every child will go on to higher education but, at the same time, we must cater as best we can for those who will. A school with a good academic reputation is invariably good also teaching Art, Music, Crafts and Sports. But whatever is taught must be well taught, high standards must be set, teachers must communicate their own enthusiasms to the children. Many children are browned off by lackadaisical teachers, they respect teachers who 'know their stuff' and who make demands on them. Even children who are not particularly academically successful respect proper teaching and learning. You could say that a champion football or baseball team is elitist: the members of the team work hard together to produce an excellent team. So by their dedication and personal commitment teachers produce a first-class school for the benefit of the children."

"Was that the reason for the success of the middle schools?"

"Precisely, dedicated teachers but also small classes, usually not more than 15, a relatively small curriculum with a thorough grounding in each subject. You know, in the former Basel Mission days the standard of Maths and English was very high."

"What are your plans for staffing?"

"I have found a splendid Headmaster in Kwesi Akuffo who graduated in English and History at St. Andrews, Scotland, his Deputy will be Grace Amponsa who studied African History and Music in London and there will be three Ghanaian graduate teachers, I don't know who they will be yet, I have asked for volunteers. Then there is yourself and Ben Berricombe from England."

"Who is Ben?"

"Like you, he is a volunteer with the Voluntary Service Organisation from Great Britain; a graduate in Maths and Music at Exeter and who like you has a Ghanaian grandparent who came from Berekum, Ashanti. I'm also in touch with a young woman who has graduated in Business Studies in Kumasi, her name is Abenaa Macdonald Bonsu."

"How did she get a Scottish name?"

"I suppose I can tell you, she makes no secret of the fact that her father was, or is still, an officer in a Scottish regiment, her mother lives near Sunyani. There is also just a possibility that the school may get the services of another expatriate from Britain who has studied Agriculture."

"Where will the money for salaries and housing and buildings come from?"

"A good question. I've been fortunate in that respect. The chief and the Local Council are fully behind the project: they have allocated to the new school a former Basel Mission

House on a large site and they will build and furnish a teaching block as well as assisting in other ways. Central Government pays salaries, gives grant for some new buildings and transport but as our enrolment will be small, certainly for some years the per capita grant will be modest and we shall have to charge fees. All secondary schools have to do that but we'll keep them as low as we can."

"What does the former Basel Mission House look like?"

"You find them wherever the Mission had a permanent station. They were large for their time, about 25 by 10 metres, built always east-west so the sun's rays never reached the walls, the walls are built of local stone up to a height of three metres then came the upper floor of timber roofed with wooden shingles and later with corrugated iron sheets. The stone walls were plastered with swish and whitewashed. Each floor had four to six large rooms surrounded by a wide wooden veranda; the living rooms were upstairs and the front and rear of the house faced onto large quadrangles flanked by outbuildings and gardens. In that space you have accommodation and storage for five or six persons. There's piped water and electric light and the bathrooms have been modernised. You will be the first along with Grace to move in and check that everything is OK.

"Then both of you will help Kwesi with the curriculum planning, timetable and a host of other things that you teachers know all about. I'm very lucky to have you three experienced teachers to deal with all the basic planning."

"How did you decide on the name of the school?"

"As you can imagine, that caused a lot of discussion but finally one of the town elders came up with the name, Brong Ahafo High School, which seemed to satisfy everybody.

There's still a lot to be done: the place is swarming with builders, joiners and painters and you may have to accept some inconvenience at the start but everbody is keen to meet the opening deadline in mid-January. I shall come up every week-end. I am a personal friend of the chief, Nana Oduro Panyin II, and I often stay with him. We got to know each other in Kumasi where he worked as a lawyer before he was installed chief. It was he who finally persuaded me to go ahead and who assured me of his fullest support. Of course, the Town Council is aware that a secondary school serving the district can be a big asset to the town and they were glad to have me to press their case with the Education Department, so we are sure of full backing."

Thelma was truly intrigued by his enthusiasm and by the modest way he spoke. It was much too early to make judgments but she felt certain that she had made a wise decision. She told him of her special interest in Ghana, about her great-grandmother Afua and how she had finally volunteered with the Peace Corps. Never before had she felt so completely at ease in talking to someone about her African background.

Tom nodded his head in agreement and understanding as she spoke.

"You may not be able to trace Afua personally but you will be able to experience the background in which she grew up, things haven't changed so much in the past hundred or so years. In the school holidays, maybe at Easter you could visit Cape Coast, Elmina and Moree; the castles and the fishing villages remain much as they always were."

He thought how lucky he had been to recruit Thelma and Ben, both with ancestors in Ghana, both well-qualified and well-motivated, it seemed that he had taken a large step forward to the achievement of his goal. Not only that, talking to Ben and Thelma had made him aware that he had found new friends with whom he had much in common. They were nearing the outskirts of Kumasi now and passing the university, there was one thing he hadn't mentioned.

"It would be a big advantage in your work if you found time to learn enough of the language for everyday use. I've already spoken to Ben about that. I can't demand it of you, only request it. In any case all the classroom teaching is in English but people here are always delighted to know that you have taken the trouble to learn some Twi. It's a tonal language and you will pick up the modulations best if you sit in the primary school classes with the young children and hear them read from their textbook. Kwesi will be able to arrange it for you and give you time off once a week."

"I'll look forward to that, it will be a thrill to get to know the language that Afua spoke."

They came to a stop in the large quadrangle of the former Basel Mission House. "Now you will hear your first important Twi word, in Ghana, *akwaaba* means welcome!" announced Tom with a smile.

5

Chapter

⚘ Nana Oduro Panyin II ⚘ and Tom McKenzie

"Oyonko mu wo oyonko." (Among friends there is one special friend). Twi Proverbs, C.A.Akrofi , Macmillan, London, 1958.

Not long after his appointment as manager of schools in the Ashanti Region, Tom and his assistant, Kwabena Mensa, were making their slow way on foot along a forest bush path in total darkness apart from the feeble light of a pocket lamp, to attend a meeting with the elders of a group of cocoa-farm villages called Akurokese located in a fertile valley south of Sunyani. The settlements were strung out along the banks of a small river and at one point where the river made a cataract, a large, deep pool had formed near which was the largest village of about thirty or forty swish houses roofed with thatch. This was Akurakese which had a store selling items like sardines, corned beef, lamps, kerosene, enamel bowls, pans, cheap cutlery, cube sugar and flour. There was a market once a week and behind the village was a well-beaten track up a scarp to the dirt road to which the cocoa-beans were head-loaded for transport to Kumasi.There were now enough children to merit a school and Tom had responded to the invitation of the chief and the elders to discuss the matter.

The entire area was covered in dense tropical forest, a thick mass of towering trees and shrubs, so that without a cutlass you could not move from the footpath. Even at noon there was deep shade but after sunset it was pitch-dark so that you could not see your hand before your face and you made your slow way along a narrow, seemingly endless tunnel. Whenever a cobweb, or leaf or liana stem brushed against your face, you felt a moment of dread. Occasionally the path was wider where cocoa had been planted and here the low shrubs had been cleared but the lofty trees like the odum, the silk cotton with its red flowers, the tulip tree, the golden cassia and a whole variety of palms had been left because the cocoa trees, which grow to heights of three metres, need their shade.

Kwabena led the way with his pocket lamp, one hand stretched behind him at intervals for Tom to touch; once Tom stumbled over a tree root but Kwabena was quick to turn and hold him as he fell forwards.

We set off in the Chevrolet truck too late and the puncture had also delayed us, somehow we have to get through the next two miles. Maybe we should have tried to send a message that we would arrive late. Tom was thinking.

The only sounds to be heard were the endless, stacatto chirp of the cicadas which pierced your eardrums, the croaking chorus of the frogs and toads, and then at intervals, the terrifying shrieks of the hyrax or tree-bear which come in a succession of screams up the scale and then die away on a top C. All at once Kwabena clutched Tom's arm.

"I think I can hear voices, maybe they are coming to find us."

Sure enough, there was suddenly the assuring flicker of hurricane lamps and the murmur of conversation followed by a meeting and cheerful calls of 'Akwaaba!' Soon afterwards, a camp fire came in sight around which the elders and the villagers were assembled, introductions were made, they were given hot tea and taken to adjoining huts where a pail of warm water, drinking water, camp beds and blankets stood ready. Later they were regaled with a meat stew, kenkey and fried plantain after which there took place the more formal welcome. Tom delighted them in giving thanks for their reception and for sending helpers to meet them by quoting the well-known proverb: *"W'asem ba a, na wuhu w'adofo ne w'atamfo"* (When you are in real trouble, you see your real friends).

The following day was taken up in discussions: school site, buildings, number of children, payment and housing of teachers, finance of the project. Tom was favourably disposed, cocoa farming had brought a certain prosperity to the area, there were many migrant farmers from Akim and Akwapim as well as from Ashanti and there were families living in the villages all the year round. Their food plots were nearby where yams, coco-yams, cassava and maize grew together with a variety of fruits and vegetables, all signs of permanent residence and the possession of resources to support a school. After the evening meal the talking had gone on animatedly when without warning Tom was struck by a fierce frontal headache together with a feeling of weariness and aching in his limbs. He said goodnight as politely as he could, hurried over to his hut, swallowed extra Paludrine tablets, dragged off his clothes and lay on the camp bed. He felt certain that it was the onset of malaria; he had taken his daily dose of tablets regularly but maybe he had been infected by a new strain of mosquito. Sure enough, within a few minutes the feverish shivering began, he wrapped the blanket tight around himself but still his entire body shook uncontrollably. After a time, the trembling gave way to a profuse sweating and this sequence was repeated a few times and he began to hallucinate. He was back as a young man in the manse in the north-west of Scotland where his father, Rev. Dr. Ian McKenzie was the minister of the Free Kirk, his mother had died of tuberculosis when he was twelve. The gaunt, lean unsmiling face of his father loomed over him, the epitome of Calvinistic piety that spoke of a stern, exacting life in which all pleasures were suspect, laughter was almost taboo, high seriousness pervaded everything; a life over which God ruled as a stern taskmaster, even the smallest duty must be performed to his glory, all was plain living and high thinking. Behind his father stood Isabel his girlfriend at university who came of a Catholic family. Their mutual love had overwhelmed them and they had planned to marry. She was trying in vain to say something to him but his father was speaking in his ministerial voice.

"I have remarked that during recent vacations you have been receiving regular letters postmarked Ullapool. The handwriting on the envelopes seems to be that of a female. You have made no mention of these letters to me. I never thought that there would be anything unspoken between us, kindly explain."

He had done so. His father's face had clouded with wrath.

"Am I to understand that you seriously intend to marry a woman of the Roman Catholic persuasion? Are you not aware that I consider the Catholic Church to be profoundly in error? Is it not clear to you that I could never tolerate such a marriage?"

"Truthfully, Father, neither Isabel nor I think that the differences between the churches to be so important."

"I had thought that after your university studies you would attend our seminary and follow in my footsteps as a minister."

"There is no hope of that."

Dr. McKenzie had abruptly left the room. A week or so later he spoke to Tom again.

"I am just returned from Ullapool to inform you that your romantic attachment to Miss Isabel Farquharson has been finally terminated," and strode away to his study.

All Tom's attempts to contact Isabel failed and no letter ever came from her, he had left home and after graduation had trained as a teacher and some years later got a post in Ghana.

It took two days for the fever to abate and he slowly surfaced into consciousness with a pleasant sensation of being well again but weak. As he opened his eyes he gazed into the smiling face of the woman who was sitting by his bed; she took his hand in hers.

"*Yeda Nyame ase, wo ho aye wo den koraa,*" (We thank God that you are really well). She handed him a calabash bowl of warm goat's milk to drink and smiled contentedly as he drank deeply. Nothing had ever tasted so good, it was as though each sip imbued him with renewed life. She called her friend softly and together they bathed him in warm water, dried him and wrapped him in a fresh blanket. He still felt feeble but the fever had gone. For two days the women ministered to him, the elders had visited him and Kwabena had discussed with him the main points of the meeting.

The whole experience became a turning point in his life, it was as if he had been incorporated into Akan life. The people of Akurakese had treated him as one of themselves and it seemed to him a confirmation that his life's work lay among them. During his fever there had been a rota of women by his bedside so that he had never been left alone in a deep sleep or in an unconscious state his personality-soul (*sunsum*) could wander about, someone must watch and wait for its return. And they had kept vigil and had welcomed him with joy back into the world. He must share this experience with Nana. The nightmare dream of his father showed how deep the emotional shock had been, he had never really forgotten Isabel and no woman had ever taken her place. He had never fully known what had happened except that on the death of his father he had found a letter from her father in which was the sentence: "Isabel has accepted my view that a marriage with your son could not succeed." But why had she never written to him? Perhaps that had been part of the decision. So wife and family had played no part in Tom's life, their place had been taken by his work in Ghana to which he now felt more committed than ever. His studies of Akan customs and belief and his skill in the language had equipped him ideally in his present post.

The friendship between Nana and Tom had begun in Kumasi where they had both served on the same regional Education Committee. Kweku Anan Oduro had been a lawyer then and when he had become chief with the title,

Nana Oduro Panyin II and had moved to Bechemantia, Tom had become a regular visitor there. It was in conversation that Nana had first mentioned to Tom the idea of a secondary school in the town and they had together first discussed the possibility of the project. Before the enstoolment, Tom had asked him:

"Why was it seemingly impossible for a chief to be a Christian and for the whole community to accompany him?"

"You know, Tom, that I have always been sympathetic towards Christian belief and attend a church service on occasion but as chief you must accept the traditional framework that binds all your people together, the chief is the intermediary between the ancestral spirits in the world beyond and those living on earth here and now, between the living and the departed, that's the vital factor for everbody. So on becoming chief, I must swear the traditional oaths to serve my people in the traditional way. I must wear traditional dress, I must pour libations in the stool house where the blackened stools of my ancestors lie and when I pray in public I must call on Nyame, Mother Earth (Asase Yaa), and the spirits of the ancestors, (Asamanfo). Every Adae day I have to honour our forbears and pray for their help and once a year at the Odwira thanksgiving and cleansing festival I pray for their continued help to all of us and pour out on the earth a libation of wine. I'm praying then for all my people, non-Christians and Christians alike. I thought at one time that I might reform the practice of praying to different gods at libation pouring but the elders wouldn't accept that, so in the end I agreed to become chief because by so doing I can bring about necessary improvements in the town. I become guardian of traditional belief but I take the remnant of my Christian belief with me!" They both laughed and Tom asked further.

"What's the religious situation like now after more than 150 years of Christian missions?"

"About half my people belong to different Christian churches: Presbyterian, Methodist,Anglican, Catholic, or to more recent arrivals like Adventists, Mormons, Witnesses, Zion, Pentecostal groups and Musama Disco. Then there are the traditional Abosom cults to which people go mainly for healing and for protection against witchcraft. There's no shortage of religion in the town whether indigenous or imported. You understand Tom, we Africans live in this world and in the unseen spiritual world at the same time, there are unpleasant things and influences to be guarded against. What unites them all is the basic traditional scheme of which the chief is the custodian and, unfortunately, the missionaries never really appreciated that fact. They thought that a chief who was well-acquainted with Christianity could simply abolish everything that they considered obnoxious like praying to different gods and to the ancestors, like sacrificing animals, pouring libation,and swearing sacred oaths. It took centuries in Europe for that to happen."

Tom thought when all the staff of the new school are together I'll ask Nana to meet them informally and answer questions on the background of Akan belief and custom. He hoped that Nana's health would continue to be good but he recalled a recent visit when Nana had confided certain anxieties to him. They were sitting upstairs in his study room; around the walls were framed photographs of special occasions in the town's history: a visit by the Chief Commissioner of Ashanti in pre-independence days, a durbar scene with all the figures in regalia, an Odwira procession, a large framed portrait of President Kwame Nkrumah and facing him demurely across the room a picture of Queen Elizabeth II on horseback. They had drunk each other's health in a gin and tonic and Nana had joked.

"I sometimes think that the organisation of the British Empire was lubricated by gin and tonics! We Ghanaians often wondered what motivated your people on a far north-western island of Europe to establish colonies all around the world!" Tom rejoined in the same vein.

"Scotch whisky and soda at sundown may also have had a similar function!"

Nana drew his chair nearer and looked directly at Tom.

"How long have we known each other, Tom?"

"It must be five or six years now."

"I need to confide to you something that I can't discuss with my elders or with the Queen Mother yet, I have some kind of illness."

"What form does it take?"

"When I awake my entire body feels rigid and stiff, then I begin to tremble and the muscles of my limbs start to ache, it's not so painful but I have to move very slowly and carefully until I can move my arms and legs comfortably again. During the day the annoying thing is that I get tremors in both hands, the right more than the left."

He laid both hands, palms down, on the table and as he raised them his long, slender fingers began to tremble slightly.

"If I grip anything the trembling stays under control but you realise that writing and handling anything is difficult. Then I get often a feeling of tiredness and a lack of ability to concentrate. Have you any knowledge about this kind of illness?"

"No, only that chronic arthritis can affect the muscles. Have you consulted a doctor?"

"I can't do that privately because I'm a public figure, the elders have to know and then there's all sorts of speculation, that I've been bewitched for example." Tom thought hard.

"Let me drive you one day to the hospital at Agokro. I know the surgeon there who can examine you privately and give you a diagnosis. After that you can decide to speak with your elders." And that was what they had done. All the symptoms pointed to one cause: Parkinson's Disease, a kind of paralysis which causes muscular spasms and tremors and for which there is no known cure. The surgeon was, however, encouraging and optimistic there were tablets to minimise the tremors, massage at the start of the day would help the muscle-tone, in short the illness was a disability not a threat to life. Nana had convinced his elders that he was able to fulfil all his duties and he grew skilful in concealing the trembling in his hands on public and ceremonial occasions while his 'soul' – a young boy who sat at his feet or behind his chair – handed things to him in a way that he could grasp them. Nothing more was said and Tom admired the courageous way that Nana triumphed over his disability.

On another occasion after they had attended the wedding reception of a mutual friend Kweku had asked Tom:

"Tom, my friend, why have you never married? You have

lived a long time alone. Do you never feel the need of a wife, of children, of the warmth of a family?"

Tom was silent for a few moments. He'd never told anyone the full story, who better than Nana, his closest friend, to hear it?

"At university I met a fine young woman, Isabel Farquharson by name, with whom I fell deeply in love and she with me, and for two years we were inseparable. Her family was Catholic and my father was a Protestant minister, narrow-minded and bigoted, who ruthlessly opposed the affair and persuaded her parents that a marriage between us would be a disaster. He forbade me to see her and her parents must have said the same to Isabel. I tried to contact her in vain. It was only many years later on the death of my father that I had to fly to Scotland to sort out the contents of the house, when by the purest chance I found a few letters held together by a rubber band addressed to my father, one from Isabel's parents to say that they had disowned her, but the last two letters were addressed to me in Isabel's handwriting, one postmarked Ullapool and the other, almost two years later, postmarked Glasgow. On both envelopes she had written "Please forward," but he had opened them and had presumably read them.

You can imagine my feelings, Nana, holding letters from the woman I had promised to marry, letters that were now at least seven years old! I sat down on a packing case with a beating heart and unfolded the first letter: it was quite short and informed me that she was pregnant and was in deep disgrace with her parents; the second was longer to say that her life at home had become intolerable and that she had left her parents to live alone in Glasgow and was working in a department store. Now, in a month's time she would sail with an immigrant, assisted-passage group to Australia with her baby boy that she had named Thomas. She ended the letter with words that I know by heart: "I know that you will have written to me but my parents have never given me the letters, they speak only of my disgrace. Oh, my dear, dear Tom, what have we done to deserve this fate? Think of me as I shall ever think of you."

"Have you ever tried to trace them?"

"Yes, but without success. I went to Ullapool but the family had moved; I tried the University Registration Office but they had no information. There was simply no clue at all. I think that she might have changed her name, don't forget that the trail was eight years old. So you see, I have a son somewhere who has never seen his father and whose mother made the mistake of falling in love with me. Perhaps we were both victims of parental prejudice. But that's why I have never since considered marriage.

"Perhaps I overreacted: I never spoke of my father again, I lived for my work and became a self-imposed loner. I felt guilty for what had happened to Isabel and the boy and I couldn't do anything to remedy their situation, but in addition I can see now that in avoiding any future commitment to a woman it was because I didn't want to be hurt or to hurt someone I loved."

Nana nodded sympathetically and said:

"I can understand your feelings, Tom, but I think that after all these years you can bury this unpleasant experience; circumstances were too hostile for you both. You should take a wife now, I'm sure that there are many fine women who would jump at the chance of sharing their life with you."

They smiled at each other and raised their glasses in salute; their friendship had been deepened and Tom reflected on Nana's words. They shook hands warmly and Tom drove away.

Chapter

❧ *The Opening of the High School* ❧

"Education is what survives when what has been learned
has been forgotten."

Professor B.F.Skinner, "New Scientist", 21 May 1964.

Nana and Tom had long ago agreed that the opening
date for the school should be in the first week of
January 1964 on a Saturday and somehow the
major difficulties had been overcome and the staff were in a
position to make a start. The basics were in place: chairs and
tables in classrooms with blackboards and some pictures on
the walls; there were books and writing materials available
but, above all, there were trained and experienced teachers
ready and waiting. For a week now the harmattan dry wind
had been blowing steadily from the north; the normal high
humidity had been replaced by a parching dryness that
sucked the moisture from the skin and from the eyes and
lips, the air felt cold, the dust in the atmosphere obscured the
sun, wooden tables and doors warped and cracked and all the
vegetation turned brown except for the palms and the forest

trees. But at least you could plan with certainty for a ceremony outdoors, it wouldn't rain or be too hot and sticky; and so in the front quadrangle of the old Basel Mission house a raised platform faced rows of benches and seats with standing room all round. All was set for the guests for the formal opening of the Brong Ahafo High School.

Nana and his elders had walked in a small procession preceded by a pair of dono drummers who carry the drums under the left arm and beat out a walking rhythm. The okyeame was there holding his official staff of office while the queenmother was accompanied by a small group of women attendants who wore a colourful matching outfit of headscarf, blouse and skirt. Nana looked every inch a king in his royal robes: he wore the eye-catching gold and blue patterned silk toga in the design called *adweneasa* a word by which the artist weaver meant 'my skill is exhausted'. It is an intricate design with a mixture of gold, blue, green and red silk threads in lines and stripes. In former days only the Ashanti king could wear this pattern; it has a royal air about it; heavy and lustrous, it covers the entire body leaving only the right shoulder free in the fashion of classical Rome. Because he was of above average height he wore the ntama to advantage although he stooped a little; he was spare in form, courteous and composed. A fillet of aggrey beads encircled his temples and round his neck he wore a finely-wrought gold chain, on his right arm was a gold bracelet which flashed as he walked. As the group arrived at the gate, the drummers beat out a special flourish, the call *'Agoo'* was made and answered by the Headmaster, *'Amee'* (You may enter).

All the guests stood and applauded until Nana and the

queenmother were seated in their brass-studded ornamental chairs which had been carried from the *ahemfie*. There were representatives from all the religious and social groups in the town as well as delegates from Government and from the Asanteman Council and from neighbouring towns occupying the benches and chairs. All around stood townsfolk and school children. After a prayer by one of the ministers the proceedings began: Tom McKenzie gave a formal welcome to those present and then addressed Nana through the okyeame in traditional Akan style and introduced the staff of the new school one by one, Ghanaian and expatriate, stating their country of origin, their home town, their teaching experience and qualifications. Each one received warm applause; never before in the town had there been such a gathering of competent young people for service as teachers. Tom concluded by requesting Nana to give them full support. After each few sentences he paused for the Okyeame to 'interpret'. Barima Yao Gyamfi took full advantage of the occasion: as spokesman for the chief he was one of the senior elders; he was proud of his deep, resonant voice and his fluent command of the language so he made an oratorical display to which everyone listened in appreciation. He wasn't translating in the linguistic sense, they all understood the language, but he expressed what was said in an elevated style. Nana praised all those who had helped to bring the school into being and spoke of the vital role the school would play in the future. He was handed a pair of scissors, took a few steps forward to where a ribbon in Ghanaian colours had been stretched across the main entrance door of the new classroom block and cut the ribbon with the words:

"I cut this ribbon to declare the new school to be open,

and I give it the name, Brong Ahafo High School; may success attend all those who teach and all those who learn within it."

The visitors were then free to wander around and to take refreshments after which they filed past Nana and his group to take their leave and to put their contributions and their promissory notes in the collection box. It was clear that the project had found full approval.

As Tom and the Headmaster escorted Nana back to the Ahemfi, Tom begged a final favour.

"Do you think that it would be a good idea Nana, if you as patron of the school, could give a talk to the school staff in which you could outline your hopes for the school and allow a few questions from the staff? They would all appreciate that." Nana at once agreed and as a result on the following Saturday they were invited to the *ahemfie* to a meal of savoury stew, fufuu and fried plantain, followed by a huge bowl of fresh fruit salad. At table, Nana chatted with them and when the meal was finished they moved into a reception room where Nana began his talk.

"It was Dr McKenzie's wish that I should tell you of my hopes for the school. I would say briefly that in this intense transition period for our country all our schools have a great part to play; we are living in two worlds at the same time: our traditional life is confronted by the western technological world. We are trying to make the best of both but that means that in agriculture, in commerce, in social customs, in politics, in religion—in every part of our lives we have to make compromises and it is only in the schools that our children can learn to cope with these problems. I won't say anything more at this stage because I shall be able to enlarge on this theme in answer to your questions."

Grace spoke first; she was deputy head and Kwesi had nodded encouragingly to her. She was attractive by any standards: tall and slim she held her head erect above her slender neck; she looked cheerful and good-natured in repose and when she smiled,which she often did, she radiated an air of inward contentment that made you feel good, made you feel that you wanted to be her friend. She appeared capable too: in all sorts of ways her colleagues had come to rely on her good advice and helpfulness.This evening she was wearing African dress, a royal-blue tie-dyed short-sleeved blouse with white lace embroidering the collar, a matching skirt and sandals. She belonged to one of the leading families in Bekwai where her uncle was Gyasehene and since her return from her studies in London she had been under pressure to marry and to take a full part in the traditional life of the town. But Grace liked her job and she had done well in her career; she had taught in the girls' secondary school in Aburi and now had been promoted to deputy head in a school nearer home. More than once she had thought that if she married a white man it would be much easier for her to combine career and family. And then on one never-to-be-forgotten day she had heard the music of Mozart outside the open door of Ben's room. She had stood quite still, transfixed by the serene clarity of the melody: it was part of Mozart's Clarinet Concerto in A Major. She had tapped on his door and he had said 'Come in'; she tip-toed in, took a cushion and without speaking sat on the floor. They both listened to the end of the tape and only when the plaintive final notes of the clarinet had died away Ben had said:

"It's one of my favourite pieces of Mozart. You know,

Grace, I learned to play the clarinet at university, not particularly well, I'm afraid, but it has come to mean a lot to me."

And Grace had replied with shining eyes:

"Like me at Westfield College when I studied Music and learned to play the violin."

Ben shyly took out his clarinet from its case, handled it affectionately and gave it to her.

"I haven't played it in Africa yet."

She returned it to him, ran upstairs and came back with her violin and then from the score that Ben had, they had played the melody from the adagio together. They had laughed over their frequent mistakes and started again and again until they got it right. They had looked at each other completely entranced and Ben remarked:

"There's something deeply moving about that melody that I can't express in words. My music tutor in Exeter used to say about it that if after you died you awoke and heard it you would know that, after all, you had reached the right place."

"I feel that too; with just a few notes Mozart transports you to a new world."

From that moment Grace and Ben had been engrossed in talk about classical music, their favourite pieces, composers and orchestras: all Ben's shyness fell away and whenever afterwards they had the time, they had listened and had played their instruments together. Both were aware that through their mutual love of classical music their affection for each other was deepening; music became literally for them 'the food of love' as Shakespeare once described it. Ben talked more freely with Grace than he had ever done before with anyone and Grace let him speak about himself, his ideas and his interests; she knew intuitively that that was what he needed, to find expression for his thoughts and feelings. And one day, as they listened to Mozart's Magic Flute, Ben took her hand and pressed it to his lips. It was enough, they were at once in each other's arms, at first not speaking but looking with wonder into each other's eyes until their lips met.

All this flashed through Ben's mind as he looked proudly at Grace putting the first question to Nana; that he would fall in love with a Ghanaian girl had never before crossed his mind. How kind and capable and loving she was! He would never forget the day when she had tiptoed into his room and they had listened in rapt silence to Mozart; he fancied that he could see Mozart smiling about what his music had kindled in their hearts!

"What interests many of us, Nana, is how we can work out a formula for coping with the transition period that we are living in. We have our traditional religion and customs on the one hand and Christianity and western civilisation on the other. How can we adjust ourselves to two cultures? What part can our schools play?"

"That's a very good qestion to start with," said Nana, with a smile.

"Here in West Africa we are confronted by two world religions, Christianity and Islam, each of which asserts that their God is the only supreme god and their holy book the only true moral code. As everyone knows, I am sympathetic towards Christianity but I have never been able to accept the view that one expression of religion possesses all the truth. Long before Christianity and Islam existed there were many other religions like Judaism, Buddhism and the religions of ancient Egypt, of Persia, Babylon and Rome. And before them, there existed the so-called nature religions like those of the Akan, for example. We have our high gods like Nyame, Asase Yaa, the Earth Mother; we have the lesser spirits,the abosom; we believe that our ancestors in the next world take a continual interest in our welfare in this world; we believe that there are good and bad spiritual, invisible forces that can seriously affect our everyday lives. We have our own laws: acts and deeds that can harm the community are forbidden while our ancient customs seek to keep us on a even path. Now, what always amazes me is the fact that Christian missions from the 18th century and later Moslem missions made no attempt to relate their religious message to Akan religious thinking, they just condemned all of it as misguided, primitive and even repulsive. Converts had to separate from their community, and from family and kinsfolk if they became Christian or Moslem.

Of course, our people were quite impressed by the white man and his material achievments: he had huge ships, wheeled vehicles, large houses, he could read and write, he built schools and his medicine men were skilful. No wonder that our people inferred that the white man's gods and spirits must be powerful and that the secret of the power lay in the book called the Bible. We Africans are not prejudiced against any other religion, each one has something good in it, and if that can bring security in a hostile world, or bring remedies for sickness, or offer hope for the future, then we are prepared to accept it. And that's what we did: we accepted the Christian religion but we never gave up our allegiance to our family group and never gave up the generally-accepted framework of Akan thinking. In my case, I was educated in mission schools and learned a lot about the Bible but I never became a member of any church and when I became chief I became the guardian of the traditional religion of my people but I took many Christian ideas with me!

"Then, as you all know, the world has been completely changed by technology and we in West Africa are involved in that change: we want tarred roads, water and electricity in our homes, we want radio and television, hospitals and schools, we want modern transport facilities and there's no way that we can avoid the changes that these amenities bring with them. So Grace is quite right, how can we adjust and teach our children to come to terms with the modern world without losing those elements in our indigenous life that we consider most valuable? I studied European law systems which are based on private land ownership; in Africa land belongs to the community so that we have been forced to adapt. In Ghana, the Akan peoples have a matrilineal system of inheritance which gives our women a status in the community that they do not have in Moslem societies and still do not have in many Christian countries. Now Grace asked: how can we deal with such problems? There's no easy answer but the only places where these matters can be discussed are in the high schools, colleges and universities as well as in councils and parliaments. A great responsibility rests with teachers at every level."

They were all impressed by the cogent and clear way, in excellent English, the chief spoke. Abenaa put up her hand to ask:

"What particular Akan beliefs and customs were most disliked by the Christian missionaries?"

In reply, Nana ticked them off on his fingers: They were

polygamy, swearing oaths, praying to ancestors and to different gods, praying to and pouring libation to Mother Earth
and to human and animal sacrifices. Let me comment on
these in turn. Throughout history having more than one wife
at the same time was a standard feature of royalty and of
wealthy men; the taking of concubines posed no problem
and in many lands this social arrangement still holds. Now
the Christian missionaries came mostly from countries where
the ideal of lifelong monogamy was very strong and where
divorce was difficult and costly. It isn't so today, attitudes
have much changed. But a century ago no chief could
become a Christian without sending all his wives away except
one. There have been chiefs who would have liked to
become Christian but plural wives was always the stumbling
block. So far as I know, no chief in Ghana has ever been
accepted as a convert and the churches exist in our communities as separated groups. Otherwise, as in the Middle Ages
in Europe, whole communities could have been baptized.

"The swearing of oaths as a necessary beginning of a
process in a court of law is universal in all countries. What
the missionaries never seem to have understood was that
among the Akan peoples the oath was primarily an oath of
allegiance to the chief, like in feudal times in Europe, and at
the same time an oath of loyalty to the state. So that the only
way that you could start a legal process for adultery, theft,
slander, abuse, assault, inheritance and such cases was to
swear the 'forbidden' word which every Akan community
has. The case had then to be heard otherwise the solidarity
of the community was in danger. The oath was not at all a
wrongful use of God's name.

"When Akans pray we address the supreme God under

one or other of his names, or we invoke the Earth Mother as the source of life, or we make requests to the ancestors, the Asamanfo, who are deeply concerned with what we are doing, or we call on the help of one or other of the invisible spirits, the Abosom, which inhabit rivers, great trees and rocks. You see, as Abenaa well knows, we Africans live in two worlds at the same time, this material one and the invisible one: there are always unseen forces at work that can cause illness, misfortune and accidents. That's why we are always searching for security and freedom from these things. I have always found it difficult to understand why Christians object when they themselves pray to God in three persons, when they call on the help of the saints and make a special remembrance of their dead.

"Animal and human sacrifice has had a place in religion since the beginning of human history: the reason isn't far to seek. If you ask God to do something for you, you have to show that you mean what you say by bringing a gift of some kind, something of real value to you like a fowl or a goat or a sheep. When the blood is shed, you can't take it back. When human life is offered, it is the supreme sacrifice. Of course, you can't bargain with God in that way, but it's natural to think so; remember the Bible story of Abraham and Isaac. It was easy to be highly critical of the killing of people at the death of a chief but it was also unthinkable to send a chief to the ancestors without servants. The custom was rightly abolished by the British but you must recall that for Africans death on such an occasion was a transition to another life. I sometimes feel that white people suffer from a morbid fear of death yet, by contrast, in their wars, millions of lives have been lost. In the old days in Ghana, battles lasted one day. During the war in Korea one of my elders once asked me: 'Don't the white men ever stop fighting to count their dead?'

"To sum up, I think that the missionaries came out of a Europe obsessed by their technical superiority of which their religion was a part; their culture, their commerce and industry, their Christianity, were all woven into a pattern which they called civilisation so that they rarely looked for anything of value in Ghanaian ways of life and thought. This was a time, remember, when everything was evaluated in terms of progress: even in religion there were 'early', 'primitive' religions which had been superseded by religions that were based on holy books But the final 'highest' religion was Christianity. Just think, Abenaa, how in the intervening years attitudes have changed in so-called Christian countries: easier divorce laws, equal rights for women, tolerance of 'other' faiths and different cultures; how astrology and fortune-telling flourish – the former Christian dogmatism has almost disappeared."

Nana smiled at them, poured himself a glass of water and drank gratefully; he seemed to be tired and glad of the pause.

Alastair came in last with a general question:

"I have been reading about the cocoa revolution in Ghana. How did that happen? Is cocoa still the most important export?"

Nana smiled and with the ease of a lawyer he gave them the basic facts.

"Cocoa made Ghana's fortune. We don't drink it much ourselves or eat much chocolate but the rest of the world does. It was first grown by three Basel Mission farmers in Akropong-Akuapem who reported in 1868 that they had four acres planted with cocoa and coffee. Ten years later a certain Tetteh Quarshie, a Ghanaian who had been employed in Fernando Po, brought cocoa seedlings back with him to Mampon-Akuapem. He profited by the advice of the Swiss and his plantation provided the first consignment of cocoa beans shipped by the then Basel Trading Company in 1893. This consignment of 80 pounds weight was worth two pounds, 15 shillings sterling. In Independence year 1957, 64 years later, Ghana exported 250,000 tons worth 80 million pounds sterling!

"It made a social revolution: families became prosperous and joined in the scramble for fertile forest land in Akim and Ashanti, many Akuapem farmer families migrated north. The period between 1912 and 1950 was a high point: schools and churches were built, families erected solid stone and cement-block houses, new roads were made, lorries were bought and there was a great increase in the import of consumer goods. At that time Ghana had the second highest per capita income in all Africa, second only to the Republic of South Africa. Almost 50% of world production was grown on family-owned farms of about 5 acres. There was no plantation system so that the profit from the sale of cocoa was widely distributed among the families who grew the crop. During those years, the Cocoa Marketing Board operated a system by which the farmers received half the estimated harvest value of their crop in advance; the balance being adjusted at harvest. The large European Trading firms acted as brokers and shippers of the crop. In the last few years this system seems to have broken down and some farmers are selling their crop over the border in the Ivory Coast."

Suddenly Nana's voice faltered and he stopped speaking, laid both hands palms down on the table and lowered his head. Tom darted swiftly to his side, poured out a glass of water and held it to his lips. Nana drank and allowed Tom to hold him firmly with one arm round his waist and to lead him from the room. It was clear to them all that Nana had been taken ill and they waited uneasily until Tom returned to inform them that Nana was better; he had suffered from an attack of dizziness after an exhausting day. He would not be returning to continue the session and sent his apologies. Tom passed on his request that he did not wish the incident to be discussed outside. The guests asked Tom to convey their thanks for the invitation to Nana and then quietly took their leave. When Tom went back to Nana he was sitting in his easy chair.

"It's my illness again, Tom, it's getting more difficult to keep the trembling under control. Some of my elders have been pressing me to visit the obosom priest at the shrine at Besease; they say that it is my duty to consult the traditional spirit to find out about my illness and to satisfy them I have finally agreed but I want you to accompany me. I'll let you know when the visit is arranged."

Tom had agreed and on the following Thursday he met Nana and three of the elders in Ejisu and from there they were escorted by the local chief and his elders to the shrine house. The house was built in traditional Ashanti style, made up of four rooms with raised floors and open to the front set round a central courtyard. A small door in one corner was the only entrance to the right of which was a kitchen, and as they passed into the courtyard the drummers in the room on their left sounded out a welcoming rhythm; facing them was the shrine room of the abosom partially concealed by intricate open-work screen walls. To the right stood the sacred tree – the Nyame Dua – in the forked branches of which a calabash containing pure water was wedged. At the foot of the tree the offering of Nana – a gift of money - was placed. Another room was reserved for the two women dancers and singers and here the vistors were offered seats; Nana was led to a chair on the dais of the shrine. They were formally greeted and welcomed by the obosom priest and his attendants in the name of the Obosom Ta Kora, and the proceedings began.

The drumming started again and the obosom priest or okomfo performed a series of special solo dances characterised by erratic leaps and spins until he fell into an hypnotic trance. He was then 'possessed' by the Obosom spirit and could become the mouthpiece of the spirit; he sat down suddenly on a low stool, raised his fly-whisk as a sign for his linguist to approach to interpret the voice of the spirit which he uttered in an unknown language. As he spoke he held both of Nana's hands in his own. The oracle was prefaced by the Akan proverb: *Onyame ma wo yare a, oma wo aduru,* (If God gives you the illness, he also gives you medicine) and went on to explain: this '*mmusu*' (misfortune or affliction) is sent by God and cannot be cured but there are medicines which will help Nana to fight the disease. He will live yet for many years to rule his people.

After the ceremony was over and they were travelling back, Nana asked Tom for his impressions.

"I couldn't see inside the shrine but I saw and heard everything else. It reminded me of the clairvoyant sessions led by a medium which were once popular in Europe. It was interesting because the oracle confirmed the medical doctor's verdict."

The elders nodded their heads in agreement; the tutelary spirit had endorsed the diagnosis of western medicine.

Chapter

❧ *Alastair Anderson* ❧
decides his future

Bere annu annu a, etra. (An opportunity not taken is lost).
Akan Proverb.

One of Alastair Anderson's jobs was to pick up the school mail from the post office box in town and to collect any parcels and other items. One day after the start of the new school year in January 1965 he parked the truck, greeted the letter-writer who sat on the balcony at his makeshift desk, opened the box and scooped the letters out. He saw at once that there was one addressed to him: a travel-stained brown envelope half-covered with French Equatorial African stamps and postmarked Brazzaville, the hot, humid capital city on the north bank of the Congo river. A Par Avion sticker had not helped its progress: it bore a Lagos control mark and it had been opened and re-sealed in Accra. Altogether it had taken ten days to reach its destination. The letter was from his uncle

Neil and was quite short: "Dear Alastair, after more than a year in the Congo I am on my way back to the UK via Accra. I shall arrive in Accra on the 28th by Pan Am. I should like to meet you and if possible Tom McKenzie. All good wishes, Neil."

The letter had come at the right time because he could finally discuss his uncertain future with his uncle. His permit to stay in Ghana would expire in six months and although Tom had told him that he would get permission to extend his stay on account of his work at the school he still had to resolve the problem of his long-term future. What a lousy mess-up of his life he had made so far! Here in Ghana he felt himself to be a proper person again taking a full part in a new worthwhile enterprise. He enjoyed his work at the school: he had laid out a vegetable and fruit plot, had planted a group of cocoa trees; he was responsible for school supplies and transport as well as being caretaker. He had developed an interest in cocoa-farming through Abenaa's mother's three farms which she had shown to him and had made it clear to him that if he settled down with Abenaa he could take the farms over! It was indeed a most inviting prospect but what were Abenaa's views? He got on very well with her and she with him but there was always a certain reserve between them. You could understand that; he was a comparative stranger, expelled from the university, he had no career and no qualifications, a drifter without prospects. He had always felt that he had no right at all to say anything affectionate to her. She knew very little about him or his family and you couldn't ask a girl to share your life on that basis. His aunt had encouraged him to stay a while in Ghana, now it was high time for a frank talk with uncle Neil to finalise his plans.

Kwesi was in his office and like always he stopped what he was doing to give his caller his full attention. Alastair gave him the letter to read.

"My uncle Neil is one of the leading foreign correspondents with the *London Daily Telegram*; he has been in the former Belgian Congo covering the situation there and is now on his was home. I should be grateful for permission to meet him so that he can take my personal news to my parents."

"Of course you may go; try to get Dr. McKenzie to take you from Kumasi. By the way, reporters like your uncle arriving from the Congo may be closely questioned; the *London Daily Telegram* is not favoured by the Government. If Tom is with you he may be able to smooth the way. Incidentally, I have a meeting in Accra that day and I may be able to join you later."

Alastair had lost no time in contacting Tom but as they waited at the exit-gate at the airport they saw that Neil was accompanied by two uniformed policemen who escorted him to the immigration office. Alastair and Tom stood anxiously outside the door until they were called inside. A stern-looking officer seated at a desk began by asking Neil:

"Who are these two men who have come to meet you?"

"One is my nephew, Mr Alastair Anderson and the other is the General Manager of Schools in Ashanti, Dr Thomas McKenzie."

The officer held out his hand for their passports, and turned to Neil.

"Tell me exactly what you were doing in the Congo Republic and why you wish to make a stopover in Accra."

He leaned back in his chair and listened intently to Neil's reply.

"Did you make contact with Ghanaian troops?"

"Yes, I did so on a few occasions."

"Who gave you permission to speak with them?"

"I had written permission to speak with them from the Ghana Ambassador, the Honourable Nathaniel Welbeck."

"Show me the letter."

"It is among my papers in the briefcase on the desk."

"Take it out, please."

Neil handed it to him and explained:

"I was permitted to speak with soldiers off duty in their camp in the presence of their officer."

"Did you talk with any other Ghanaian officials?"

"Yes, I was accorded a special interview by the Ghana Special Envoy, the Honourable Kojo Botsio."

"Did you send regular reports to your newspaper?"

"Yes, Sir. Two or three times a week and oftener on Important occasions."

"Did you make contact with the local people?"

"Yes, I talked with those who could speak French."

A pause ensued.

"You are no doubt aware that your newspaper is not favoured by our Government; ever since independence your paper has taken up a critical attitude towards Ghana. Why is your editor so persistent?"

"My countrymen are particularly interested in Ghana because it was the first African territory to become independent, I try always to write objectively and to present different points of view."

"We see things in Ghana from the point of view of our President. Have you copies of your reports?"

"Only of the last four, Sir."

"Take them from your briefcase and let me see them."

There was dead silence in the office while the officer opened the file and began reading. He finally looked up and asked:

"What is your view of the present situation in the Congo Republic, Mr Warner?"

"For the moment there is calm but I think that new problems will arise because the Congo is beset by so many political and tribal rivalries. The presence of Ghanaian troops has been consistently positive and helpful but I think that the United Nations Organisation has operated in a confused way and people have lost confidence in this institution; the view is widespread that it represents a new kind of colonialism. Many of the Ghanaian soldiers I spoke to wish to return home."

The was another long silence.

"How long do you wish to stay in Ghana?"

"Three days, Sir, I am also anxious to return home!"

"Where will you stay?"

"I have booked a room in the Black Star Hotel, most visiting journalists stay there."

For the first time the officer smiled.

"You reporters seem to favour the Black Star. I will give you permission to stay four days in case your plane is delayed. Try to remain always objective, Mr Warner!"

He made a note in Neil's passport, stamped it and held out his hand. The interrogation was over.

At the hotel there was a message that Kwesi would meet them at 4pm and over lunch Tom asked Neil to summarise the Congo situation for him.

"It's a tangled web, Tom, and I think it will take years to

sort it out, I can only describe some of the main threads. The three men most involved in the beginning were Patrice Lumumba, Sekou Toure and Kwame Nkrumah, all three seem to have the idea of founding a federation of independent African states not on the pattern of the USA but rather on that of the Soviet Union. Already in Guinea a one-party dictatorship has emerged and for the Congo Lumumba has the same intention. In his view Leopoldville would become the capital city of a federal socialist Africa. When Katanga seceded Lumumba made the great mistake of calling in help from the United Nations Organisation. It seemed to be a good idea but the UNO had no experience in such matters. Ghana and Guinea already had troops ready for service in the Congo but, just imagine, in a relatively short time there were 26 countries which sent 'peace-keeping' troops to deal with the civil war with Katanga! As you know, Mobotu, an officer in the Congolese Liberation Army, took over power and Lumumba was imprisoned and shot in Katanga. UN forces finally seized Elizabethville in 1963 but local revolts and rebellions, lawlessness and atrocities led to complete chaos and to an entire breakdown of law and order. All this on the background of the Cold War, with the USA and the Soviet Union waiting in the wings and Belgium still playing with the idea of keeping a grip on the mineral wealth of the Katanga province! In my view, the United Nations Organisation has been completely discredited by its handling of the Congo problem."

"Had you written much of this in the last four reports the immigration officer read?"

"Fortunately, my last reports tried to emphasise a few positive aspects otherwise they had been full of the failures of UNO and of the ineptitude of various national army contingents. Luckily he didn't ask me about my discussions with senior officers of the Ghanaian forces."

"Why was that?"

"They were all deeply discontented at the way they had been pushed around; they were seldom consulted and are highly critical of Nkrumah's policies at home and abroad. I heard that there is even a special body of troops being trained for intervention in North Rhodesia! The dissatisfaction has reached such a pitch that oppostion is being talked about."

"You mean opposition to policy in the Congo?"

"More than that. What I heard and overheard was more serious, I got the impression that only a change of government in Ghana would satisfy some of them."

"You mean, the armed forces to take over political power in this country?"

"Yes. In a one-party state there is no other possibility of change. I have no proof, I am making my own conclusion from a number of private conversations. Please do not repeat what I have said."

Kwesi had joined them and had been listening intently and said:

"That's very enlightening, Neil; we can understand much better the trend of events here in Ghana. There seems to be no end to the one-party state build-up: our press is muzzled and foreign newspapers rarely reach us, oppostion leaders like Dr J.B.Danquah and Joe Appiah have been imprisoned, the idea of a democratic opposition in Parliament is ridiculed, the country is full of advisers from Eastern European communist countries, teachers are suddenly dismissed with loss of pension, chiefs are destooled especially in Ashanti and the North, while the Convention People's Party van tours the country to check on so-called disloyalty reports made by members of the secret Circle group. Our President plays an active role on the world stage, there is talk of him going to China to discuss the situation in Viet Nam, but at home there is growing discontent with the economy, with inflation, corruption and the squandering of public money. Our President has built for himself a fortified palace on the Akuapem Ridge and bought a naval frigate from the UK which must have cost millions. Such matters are rarely subjects for debate in Parliament; formerly, even in the colonial days there was discussion about public spending. But there is much disillusionment with the way in which the Convention People's Party operates to force us all into one mould. Let me tell you what happened in the High School in Bechemantia last December.

"Without warning, a CPP combi-van came to a halt outside my office; four black-suited men got out and their leader demanded to speak with me. Ofori, my secretary, came in quickly to warn me and then led them up the stair to my office where they took seats facing me at my desk right opposite the framed portrait of Nkrumah. Ofori produced glasses and the bottle of Johnnie Walker which we reserve for special guests and I motioned him to stay so that I had a witness. There were formal greetings and we drank a toast to the President. The leader of the group spoke.

"Headmaster, we are official visitors to your school authorised by the CPP. What do you know of our party?"

"It is the political agent of the Government."

"Correct. You must know that we are pledged by our

rules to combat all ideas and groups hostile to the Government for whatever reason, tribal, neo-colonial, educational or political and you must also know that we have been reliably informed that in your school certain irregularities exist. The first has to do with the teaching of history."

He tossed a book on my desk and asked accusingly:

"Do you recognise this book Headmaster?"

"Yes. It is a History of Ghana and it is used as a text-book in this school."

"Are you aware that the writer of this book throws doubt on the view that modern Ghana is descended from medieval Ghana?"

"Yes, I am aware of that. The author says that the theory is not proven. We know that in the Middle Ages the kingdoms of Ghana and Mali fought for supremacy for a time and that finally Mali conquered Ghana but there is no evidence that any groups from Ghana wandered south-east to modern Ghana."

He laughed scornfully at me.

"What kind of evidence are you talking about?"

"I mean evidence from written records or from archaeological inscriptions to support the theory."

"Listen to me, man; since independence the CPP and our Leader have changed history and if we assert that modern Ghana is descended from ancient Ghana, that is enough proof. It is now a proven fact."

He banged his fist on my desk to emphasise his words.

"From now on this book is banned for use in your school; it is a disloyal, condescending and colonialist textbook, all copies are to be withdrawn and you will inform the Party when this has been done. The Party will not tolerate any neocolonialist teaching of African History in any school in Ghana."

He paused for effect and then asked:

"Who are your History teachers?"

"Myself, the Deputy Headmistress, Miss Grace Amponsa, and an expatriate, Miss Thelma Morrow."

"Call them now to appear at this meeting."

In a few minutes Grace and Thelma stood together at one side of the room and were introduced, When he had gone out to call them, Ofori had quickly apprised them what was afoot.

The group leader addressed Grace first.

"Where and when did you study African History?"

"At school in Ghana and at London University five years ago."

"What did you learn from the British about the name Ghana?"

Grace spoke modestly but clearly and firmly:

"I learned what the President had written in his autobiography that medieval Mali and Ghana possessed a high civilisation and that Timbuktu had exchanged teachers with the University of Cordoba in Spain. He wrote that that was an inspiration to us for the future, and added that according to tradition certain tribal groups in the then Gold Coast had links with medieval Ghana. I teach exactly what our President has written, nothing more, nothing less."

Her words couldn't have been better chosen, and her questioner played for time.

"When did our Leader write this book?"

"In 1957, the independence year."

Grace's simple and clear answer puzzled the CPP

spokesman and he needed more time to work out his response. He turned to Thelma.

"Where did you study African History?"

"At Johns Hopkins University, Baltimore, USA."

"And what did you learn there about this question?"

"Exactly what my colleague has said: medieval Ghana is an inspiration today to young people who live in modern Ghana just as in the former French Sudan they have adopted the name Mali."

He was still nonplussed and to give himself time to think he turned to me with a direct question.

"There is the second matter that has brought us here. Why have you employed an American? Do you not pursue the Africanisation programme as required by the Education Department? We are no longer prepared to pay heavily for foreigners to teach something that we can do ourselves."

"This woman teacher is a volunteer. She is a graduate trained teacher with considerable experience and is paid for by the Peace Corps of the USA; we provide only her food and accomodation."

He addressed Thelma again.

"Why did you volunteer for work in Ghana?"

"Bcause my great-grandmother was sold as a slave from this country in 1824; I wanted to offer my help and also to find out something about my roots."

The replies from Grace and Thelma set him problems that he had never before encountered and after a long pause he turned to me and said somewhat pompously:

"As a special favour we will allow you and these two teachers to teach what our President has written in his book about the change of name from the Gold Coast to Ghana."

It was a face-saving reply but also an acknowledgement of defeat. There was a pause while the four visitors took another swig of whisky. I hoped that the interview was over but the leader had still a shot in reserve, he was still trying to win a point to keep up his reputation.

"One further matter, Headmaster, you have on your staff two males from Britain. Why have you employed them? Have we not enough good teachers in Ghana?"

I felt on safe ground on this issue because the matter had been fully discussed with you, Tom.

"One of them was sent to us by the Voluntary Service Overseas Organisation in the UK: he is a trained graduate teacher of Maths and Science with good experience; he is also a volunteer and costs us nothing apart from his food and board. Moreover, his grandfather came from Berekum. The other is a student of agriculture who has a special interest in cocoa cultivation. He looks after school supplies and transport. Both have been approved by the Education Department and are on short-term contracts. In due course, to succeed them, I shall seek to recruit teachers from Ghana with similar qualifications."

There took place a whispered discussion among the four and Ofori poured out the last of the whisky for them. Finally the leader said:

"Headmaster, I accept your explanations on behalf of your staff on this occasion but I warn you that private information about your school reaches us very quickly; you should know that there are those whose loyalty to the CPP is stronger than their loyalty to you."

With that remark, they took their leave, climbed into their car and drove away. I learned later that the chief and his elders had been rebuked the previous day for their lack of enthusiasm for the government. "You see. Neil, how the situation is with us. If you write anything for your newspaper please keep names and locations out of your report." Neil replied:

"Of course, I shall fully respect your wishes. Now, would you and Tom excuse Alastair and me if we leave you for an exchange of family news."

When they were seated in another part of the lounge Neil remarked:

"You look a lot more contented than when you talked with Aunt Ruth after I had gone to the Congo; you look fitter too. What has happened in between?"

Alastair hesitated and Neil urged him.

"Just tell me the way it is with you; you know that your aunt and I have a high regard for you and we'd like to be able to assure your mum and dad that you've sorted yourself out. You can imagine how anxious they are."

"Well, first of all there's Abenaa Macdonald Bonsu, to give you her full name. I think that I've fallen in love with her."

"You mean the girl you met at Kumasi University when you first arrived in Ghana whose father is a British army officer? Your Aunt Ruth was favourably impressed by her, she seems to be an attractive, agreeable person."

"That's just it; she is a very fine person and I feel completely at home with her, she's someone I feel that I could share my life with but you see how it is: I have made an utter mess of my life so far, I have no qualifications and no permanent job. All my colleagues at the school are qualified except me, how can I possibly ask a girl like Abenaa to team up with a failure and a good-for-nothing? When I spoke earlier with Aunt Ruth about her I wasn't sure for certain about my feelings and whether I would like the work at the school so I kept postponing the decision. That's why I am speaking with you now."

"Have you told her that you have fallen in love with her?"

"No, because I feel that I'm a washout: I've nothing to offer her. I'm sure she likes me, probably out of pity, and we get on with each other OK. We both work at the High School so we see each other every day and her mother invites me for a meal from time to time. She believes that my coming to Ghana is a decision of fate; I mean, my being Scots like Abenaa's father, and that a marriage between us is written in the stars. Her mother has told me a lot about her business affairs: she has three cocoa farms that she would like me to manage and also possibly to start a small transport business. She's very shrewd but kind and sympathetic. Abenaa finds this attitude of her mother quite embarrassing and makes no comment. You can understand why. Meantime I'm only earning the salary of an unqualified teacher; I teach a few lessons of English and Maths to the lower classes but most of my time is spent in fetching school supplies, running the school vegetable and fruit farm, controlling the equipment account and being a caretaker. I have a contract at the school for two years which Tom assures me would be renewed but I can't go on indefinitely in such an unsatisfactory position let alone ask a fine girl to marry me."

"Do you like the job that you are doing or do you want to study further for something specific?"

"That's the strange thing: I enjoy my work; my colleagues, black and white, are friendly and we feel drawn together in working for the success of the school. I really like living in Ghana, not just because of Abenaa."

Neil was silent for some minutes and then said:

"Let me try to deal objectively with your problem, Alastair. First of all, you can't make plans for the future which include a young woman if you haven't told her that you love her; Aunt Ruth made that clear to you, I think. If she refuses your offer of marriage you can then decide quite independently where and how you will go on with your life; if she accepts you then you are faced with quite a different set of circumstances which Abenaa's mother has shrewdly pondered over. Her suggestions seem to me to be sound. While you are both employed at the school, you could rent accommodation; meantime learn all you can about cocoa-growing, marketing and transport. It would mean a commit-ment to a career in Ghana for some years, learning the language and becoming involved in local life. It could be that later on, especially if you have a family, you would wish to bring the estate in Scotland and your parents into considera-tion.You know that your dad hoped that you would eventu-ally take over the estate but all that can be dealt with in the future. The main thing is that you must talk with Abenaa directly you get back. If she accepts you I am sure that your aunt and I can convince your parents that your decision has been well thought out. They will only be too pleased that you have found a sensible way through after your experience at university. Let me know quite soon what has been decided and keep in touch with your parents. If Abenaa accepts you, you should consider bringing her to Sotland for a short visit!"

Alastair's eyes were bright with sudden tears of gratitude

to his uncle for the plain straightforward advice without fuss. He hastily wrote a letter to his parents for Neil to take with him and phoned Abenaa to tell her that on his return he wanted to speak with her on an important matter; he expected to come back with Kwesi the following afternoon.

Since the end of year holidays which she had spent with her mother there had been two things on Abenaa's mind: the first one was the odd behaviour of her mother when they had discussed her birthday. Her mother had been insistent that she should spend it with her at home.

"How can I ask for a day off just for a birthday? Why couldn't we celebrate it at the week-end?"

"There's a very special reason."

"What special reason can there be?"

"I don't want to tell you yet."

"Why not?"

"Because I want it to be a complete and wonderful surprise for you. Just trust me; afterwards you will thank me."

With that Abenaa had to be content. But whatever could the surprise be? She would ask Alastair, perhaps it had something to to with him. The second problem was her relationship with Alastair; she had known him now for a year and a half and since they had been both on the staff of the school she had observed his many good qualities and how well he performed his duties. She had been impressed by his ability to work with Africans, everyone who came into contact with him, liked him. He captured the interest of his pupils by his friendly encouraging manner and as caretaker he had shown his practical skills in repairs and maintenance. But, for her, there were still unanswered questions: he had never told her the full story of his expulsion from the university, he had never explained his attitude to his parents and why he had not returned home. Above all, he had never said that he found her attractive and had never uttered a word about love and marriage. It was clear that he liked being with her but he had never said so. Meanwhile at intervals her own mother showed concern at her seeming reluctance to marry. How could she possiby take the initiative with Alastair under these circumstances? She knew that he came from a well-to-do family but he had never spoken about them.

She had come so far in her regard for Alastair that she knew that if he tried to win her, he would succeed. Her mother had always impressed upon her that she had a father in Scotland and that she should learn the ways of white people, have a good education and train for a career. There had been a few approaches from families whose sons were seeking a mate but none had satisfied her mother or her. Then Alastair had arrived on the scene and her mother had been ecstatic – still was – but she had tried not to be too much influenced by her mother's enthusiasm for him. In fact, she did not want to repeat her mother's experience, to have a white man as a lover, to have a child by him but never to live with him. White people laid stress on man and wife living and sharing their lives together. On her bookshelves were a few of Jane Austen's novels which she had read, like *Emma* and *Mansfield Park*, which were full of the difficulties of young women in respectable families to find a suitable partner in life. Of course, this took place in 18th century England but partnership problems were universal and timeless. What was most desired in a man was that he should have a steady income, be well-mannered and loving; you could check on the first two but it was very difficult to be sure that a man was in love with you, especially if he never said so, you could only judge by his affectionate attitude. She had come to the conclusion that if Alastair was honest and hard-working, the sort of man who would care deeply for the welfare of his wife and children, why then she would be prepared to share her life with him, she would respect him and learn to love him. Did it matter that she was half black and half white? She thought not: skin colour didn't matter to her or to Alastair, in fact, they were both at home in Europe and in Africa.

So, since Alastair's phone-call she had been restless: it meant that he had reached a decision of some kind which would affect her deeply. All afternoon she had kept her eye on the entrance gate and as soon as the pick-up arrived she hurried out to meet Kwesi and Alastair. She knew at once by Alastair's hand-clasp and by the look on his face that the signs were good. He just said:

"Meet me in the library in fifteen minutes."

And when he came in she was sitting in the small office with two cups of Nescafe and a plate of biscuits; it was like their first meeting in the canteen at the university. Luckily they were alone, he took both her hands in his and looked in to her eyes:

"Abenaa, I have missed you very much; I realise that I have loved you since our first meeting and I now know that I want you to be my wife. If you will take me I know that we can build up a wonderful life together. That's my news from Accra, what do you say?"

It was all that she had wanted to know and she looked at him with the shining, radiant eyes that told him of her love.

"I'm so glad. Of course I will marry you. I love you too,

and I will help you to succeed in all that you plan to do."

She leaned with her head forward across the table and their lips met in their first kiss as a seal of their love. Abenaa said:

"I am so happy that this has happened but I had begun to think that you would never speak."

"I felt that I had no right to speak of love to you because I had no career, no firm prospects and no future; my uncle helped me to come to a decision. I told him about you."

Then Alastair spoke at length to her about the shambles of his student days, of his sudden decision to come to Ghana because his uncle and aunt were there, how he had felt too ashamed to return home, how working at the school had helped him through a difficult period and above all, how his relationship with her had come to mean so much to him.

"My uncle thought that your mother's plan was well planned; you could go on teaching while I got involved in cocoa farming and marketing."

"How will your parents react to the news?"

"They will accept our decision especially when my aunt and uncle explain everything to them. But they will want to meet you. I think that we should fly to Scotland at Easter."

"Do you plan to make a home in Ghana?"

"Certainly for some years. It will depend on our circumstances. I shall have to think eventually about the family estate in Scotland too; but whatever happens we shall stay together, Abenaa."

That was the reassurance that she needed and she smiled contentedly.

"Shall we tell the others that we intend to marry?" Alastair asked.

"Not yet, in school let us behave as before; let me talk to

my mother first and let us wait until you have heard from your parents. Incidentally, when is your birthday, Alastair? I don't even know how old your are; I think that I am a bit older than you. I have a birthday on the last Tuesday of this month and for some reason my mother insists that I should celebrate it with her at home; she has something planned but she refuses to tell me what it is. Has she spoken with you?"

"Not a word. Now I must think of a special gift for you!"

They kissed again and left the library into a new world that now belonged in a special way to them.

When Captain Francis Macdonald stepped aboard the British Airways plane at Heathrow he felt an astonishing sense of relief and contentment: all the legal provisions of the divorce had been completed, his son had a good position as a civil engineer, his former wife had returned to Portree and now he was on the point of flying to Ghana to join the daughter he had never seen and to be re-united with her mother he had never forgotten. At 60 he felt that the phase of his life which had begun when he had served in the army in Ghana so many years ago was now about to be completed. He had really loved Akua Bonsu and her love for him had stayed constantly in his memory. All through the intervening years he had kept this episode secret from his wife; each month, without fail, he had sent a letter and a postal order to Ghana and in return there had been letters and photographs. When his wife had discovered the deception by chance, she had been unable to forgive the fact that he had had an affair with a black woman,' as she expressed it, and the continuance of their marriage had become impossible. He had informed Akua of his divorce and she had invited him to join her for the celebration of Abenaa's birthday and to stay with her afterwards as long as he wished.

Captain Macdonald presented himself on arrival to the Immigration Officer and when he was asked:

"How long do you intend to stay in Ghana?" he found himself telling the officer the reason why he could not give a clear answer.

"I have a 25 year old daughter living with her mother in Duayaw Nkwanta in Brong Ahafo whom I have never seen. Her mother has invited me to stay as long as I like. I am retired from the army now but I served in Ghana for a time during the last war."

"I'll give you a three-month visa; if at the end of that time, you wish to stay longer, go to the Immigration Office in Kumasi, they will arrange it for you," the officer said sympathetically.

Francis took a taxi into town and booked in at the Ambassador Hotel. He had three days in which to buy a car, to check at Barclays Bank that funds had been transferred and to arrive on the following Tuesday afternoon at Akua's cottage. He decided to spend one night in Kumasi and then take the road through Nsuta and in Duayaw Nkwanta to ask his way to the house. When he did so a group of children ran excitedly ahead of him down a side road to the house; a brick bungalow with a green iron sheet roof, a large garden in front with plumbago and bougainvillea shrubs, a pawpaw and an orange tree around a lawn. His heart leaped as his glance fell on a Macdonald tartan pattern curtain in front of the open front door and on a house sign that read: Portree Cottage. Dozens of curious children's eyes watched his every movement: what had this *oburoni* to do with Awuraa Bonsu and her daughter? Francis stepped out of the car, put on his fawn light-weight jacket, locked the car and walked slowly to the front door and called out: *Agoo!* In Ghana you don't knock or ring a bell to announce your presence, Akua had taught him that, then you wait for the answer *Amee!* which means 'Come in'. The curtain was pulled aside and the two women he had come to love most in the world were standing there with welcoming smiles as they said: "Akwabaa" (Welcome!) and led him inside.

Akua spoke first. She looks still young he thought; her slim figure wearing a tasteful cover cloth and around her neck was the necklace he had given her all those years ago, the same warmth in her eyes as she held out her arms to him.

"I have waited for you and now you have come back to me!"

How simply and clearly she spoke English! She looked at him appraisingly.

"You have not changed much."

"Nor have you", Francis responded.

His thoughts raced back to the times when they had been first together and she had given a lonely soldier so much joy and contentment; so much so that he had never forgotten how happy he had been; happier, in fact, than with his wife. What a gamble marriage was! You took vows of life-long fidelity quite unaware of the way in course of time personalities change. His wife had wanted him to give up his army career and settle down in Portree as a dairy farmer but army life appealed to him, and he had welcomed his postings overseas. Then he had met Akua! He turned to the daughter he had never known as Akua proudly presented her to him:

"And now you can for the first time personally congratulate your daughter on her birthday: she is 25 today, a Tuesday child, Abenaa, but she also bears your name too!"

Abenaa wondered what she should do: embrace this man, kiss him on the lips or offer her cheeks, or simply shake his hand and smile. But this fine-looking white man was in fact her father whom she had met for the first time only moments ago; he looked much like Alastair with a youthful-looking face, ruddy complexion, crisp hair with a reddish tinge beginning to go grey, keen blue-grey eyes, clean-shaven and with the erect bearing and confident air of an officer accustomed to command. Francis sensed her hesitation and solved the problem for her by enfolding her in his arms in a tight embrace, kissing her firmly on the lips and saying:

"What an attractive young lady you have become, Abenaa! I am so proud to meet my daughter for the first time!"

She pressed him close and murmured in his ear:

"You are the father I have so longed to meet!"

They sat down together around a low table on which glasses and drinks were standing ready: first a champagne toast and as they clinked glasses their eyes shone with affection,Akua and Francis were both thinking the same: is it really possible after a lapse of 25 years to be in love again like the first time?. But Abenaa's keen observation of her parents told her that their love really had stood firm through the years. She held out her arms to them; they had given to her her life, all that she was as a person she owed to this Ashanti woman and to this man from Scotland and the three of them joined hands as a sign of the bond that united them. Then she said:

"Now, my mother and my father, I have a special announcement to make; a secret to share with you both to complete this wonderful occasion. Only a few days ago a white man from Scotland proposed marriage to me and I have accepted! My mother knows him but I hope that my father can meet him soon and give his approval. His name is Alastair Campbell Anderson, he is working at the High School in Bechemantia; his father is the Laird of Shipness in Kintyre and he was a soldier in the last war with a Scottish regiment."

She looked appealingly at her father. who said: "With all these qualifications how could I refuse him as a son-in-law? He is not a Macdonald but to be a Campbell is very good, too." Their cup of happiness was truly full; they drank more of the champagne and, holding hands they danced a three-some around the table.

All at once they were aware of the curious eyes of the children peering in through the open windows and behind them friends and neighbours from the village were beginning to arrive with good wishes for Abenaa's birthday, for she and her mother were popular figures. Could it be that this white man was Abenaa's father? All three went into the garden and the visitors listened in delighted silence as Akua told them what had happened; they all shook hands in congratulation and the visitors wished them *'Wo tiri nkwa!'* (Long life to you!), and took their leave.

Akua presided over their evening meal together and the talk never ceased. It was quite late before Francis drove his daughter back to Bechemantia.

"When am I going to meet this young man of yours?" he asked.

"I think that next Sunday you could come for us and we could spend the day together."

And that's what they did.

Chapter

♪ *A Political Crisis* ♪

"What we want is the right to govern ourselves or even to misgovern ourselves."

Kwame Nkrumah, *Autobiography*, p.164.

Sometime before Christmas 1965, Nana had invited Tom to stay with him for a few days and over a sundowner they were discussing the CPP visit to the High School.

"I suppose you heard about it from Kwesi Akuffo?" Tom asked.

"Yes. He behaved tactfully and properly; I was pleased that he avoided an open breach and that Grace and Thelma spoke up so well. You know, the elders and I had a similar visit and we were not quite so discreet. There is much discontent among cocoa farmers at the way the cocoa business has been handled by the Government and many people resent the scorn of Kwame Nkrumah for the National Liberation Party and for the Asanteman Council.

He doesn't discuss anything with us: he regards Ashanti as a remnant of feudalism and if we speak of federation it is considered disloyal. Ever since Dr Busia spoke in London before independence, Ashanti traditions and the system of indirect rule introduced by the British have been despised as undemocratic.

"What did Busia, in fact, say?"

"He was reported in the British press as appealing to the British Government to delay independence because the country was not ready for parliamentary democracy. I can quote his exact words: "We still need you(the British) in the Gold Coast. Your experiment there is not complete. Sometimes I wonder why you seem in such a hurry to wash your hands of us." Do you think, Tom, that the British will ever come back?"

"Not ever, Nana. The majority opinion in the UK is that the days of colonialism are over."

"Why didn't the British offer us a scheme like the one that the French colonies, except for Guinea, accepted?"

"I think that the British placed faith in the Commonwealth but they were not positive enough about it; besides, left-wing political opinion is very strong in the UK. Even in the Conservative party the mood was in favour of Macmillan's 'wind of change.' In any case, in Africa and elsewhere, self-rule and independence had become inevitable. But why has Nkrumah's popularity declined in Ghana?"

"I think that his pursuit of the one-party state idea is the reason. The arrests of Dr J.B.Danquah and Joe Appiah, the control of the press, the use of deportation to get rid of critics, the CPP and Circle activities, the dismissal of 'disloyal' teachers, the de-stooling of 'recalcitrant' chiefs: these things simply alienate people. We've always had freedom of speech in Ghana, even in the colonial period, now we have to be careful of what we say in public. Another factor is that people are unsure about what our troops are doing in the Congo and about the role that Ghana is playing in Africa as though it is our destiny to organise a union of African states on a Soviet pattern. There is even a rumour that a special army contingent is being trained to overthrow the Smith regime in Northern Rhodesia! We have more and more expatriates from communist countries to teach us collective farming while our own successful cocoa industry is in decline! Why have we bought a naval frigate at great cost? Do we fear an invasion from the sea? Formerly, such things were discussed, but not now. Suddenly, the coming of independence has produced a new set of political aims and an alien political atmosphere."

"Do you know Kwame Nkrumah personally?"

"I got to know him quite well during his time in London when I was studying Law. He had studied in the USA and he had the idea of doing research for a Ph.D but he gave it up because he became vice-president of the African Students' Union and was also deeply involved in political activities."

"What was his family background?"

"He belongs to the Nzima district in SW Ghana. He went to a Roman Catholic school then to the Government Teachers' College in Accra and became a teacher. Later he studied at Achimota where he was much influenced by Dr. Kwegyir Aggrey, who was the first African member of staff. He and Dr.A.G.Fraser laid the foundations of the secondary school, the training college and the university. Dr Aggrey was a Fanti from Anomabu and was a determined opponent of racial discrimination and a firm believer in racial equality. Kwame Nkrumah was greatly influenced by him and one of Aggrey's sayings was often repeated, his piano keyboard analogy: 'You can play a tune of sorts on the white keys only, and a tune of sorts on the black keys only, but to make the best music you need both the black keys and the white.' After Achimota he was offered a place at Lincoln University, then the only University in the USA open to blacks. His family was too poor to support him so he had to work at all sorts of jobs to pay his way. He told me once that he was friendly with a girl in Philadelphia who lent him money occasionally but it wasn't a love affair. He never wanted to get involved with a woman who might cause him to lose sight of his political goal. He left his books with her and years later, when he was awarded the honorary degree of Doctor of Laws at Lincoln, he called on her to collect his books."

"What was your estimation of him at that time in London?"

"He was in his middle-thirties then and was well-liked by everybody; although he was a strongly-motivated Marxist he put forward his views in a charming, persuasive way. He hated colonialism and imperialism like poison and was convinced that no colonial power would ever give a colony its independence, so he studied revolutionary methods, not just Russian, but in history, men like Hannibal, Cromwell, Napoleon, Gandhi, Mussolini and Hitler. In the end he has most influenced by the 1917 Russian Revolution backed up by a strong and dedicated political party that would rule in the name of the people. that's why he founded the Convention Peoples' Party and the organisation called the Circle whose members swore an oath of personal loyalty to his leadership."

"Didn't that cause argument?"

"I and a few others argued against his dismissal of indirect rule but, don't forget, Marxism was 'in' among the students and the triumph of Soviet propaganda was almost complete. The influence of George Padmore, the West Indian journalist, and of Harry Pollitt, the communist leader, was profound; he read the *Daily Worker* and often quoted from it. To be frank, Tom, I never thought that he would achieve his aim so easily, but he really was a dedicated and ambitious politician; he possessed a certain charisma and enthusiasm, and when he spoke so earnestly, people listened."

"Did he have many close personal friends?"

"Not so many. Kojo Botsio was closest to him, they returned to the Gold Coast from London together; they travelled to the USA and visited Liberia together and, you recall he was sent to London to appeal to the Secretary of State over the Federation issue which had been raised by the NLM. Komla Gbedemah was also near to him; he organised the youth movement and when Nkrumah was in prison he kept things going. After the election of 1954 Botsio became Minister of State and Gbedemah Finance Minister. I would say that the third close friend was Ako Adjei: he knew him in Philadelphia and again in London. He became Minister of the Interior. But basically, Nkrumah was a loner: he read a lot and although he was a good talker and enjoyed company, he told me once that there were times when he had to be alone and to 'switch-off', not talking, not listening, just thinking. He'd created the role for himself as political liberator, not only in the Gold Coast but also in all Africa, so intensely that, certainly after 1954, it became an obsession. When he left London I never met him afterwards. Did you ever meet him?"

"Yes. I met him in Akropong-Akuapem at the School for the Blind when we were trying to raise funds to rehouse the school; his wife was patroness of the school. We talked quite a while together."

"What about?"

"Mainly about the Presbyterian Church and its work. Did you know that when he was in Philadelphia he was employed by the Presbyterian Church there to carry out an intensive survey of the blacks from a religious, social and economic standpoint during which he visited over six hundred homes? He was deeply shocked by the racial segregation there. He told me that he had read a lot of theology and had even thought once of becoming a priest but that the rigid dogma of the Roman Catholic Church stifled him and that he now called himself a non-denominational Christian and a Marxist Socialist. He thought that the Christian Missions had done good work in Ghana, especially in education."

"Did you get the money you wanted?"

"Yes; he made an interesting deal. However much money we had raised by the end of the year, the Government would double it. One thing that seemed to impress him was that it was the only school of its kind in West Africa, it was founded by the Scots missionaries. In the end we had enough funds to acquire a large site and to put up modern buildings."

Nana paused and then asked:

"What's going to happen to us now? We seem to be growing poorer every day: our farmers are selling their cocoa over the border in the Ivory Coast because the price is better;

we have inflation to contend with and politically we have no say in what happens, everything is decided by the leader and the party. Is that what our people wanted when they voted for freedom in 1957? Is there no possibility of change, Tom?.

"Not much, Nana. One-party states don't envisage a change of government; the Leader can't be de-stooled or voted out, the one-party rule is regarded as permanent and unchangeable. Even if the party leader should pass away, the party remains in control and chooses the next leader. Such regimes are only overthown by force.

"Where is that force to come from?"

Tom was silent for a few moments and then he said:

"History is full of examples of an army taking over the reins of government. Think of Cromwell in England or of Napoleon in France. An army is the only organisation composed of men from all parts of the country controlled by well-educated and trained officers who are able to lead and to organise. Moreover they have the weapons and the discipline to overthrow a regime."

"Do you mean that this could happen in Ghana?"

"It could and can happen in any country when the political leaders lose the confidence of the armed forces and it can happen overnight. The army is the only force in a country that possesses the discipline and the organisation to operate on a national scale.

"Doesn't an army take-over mean civil war?"

"Not necessarily. A military coup can be bloodless because all the weaponry is its hands and it can choose the best time to act."

"You can't seriously think that such a coup d'etat could

take place here?"

"I'm always optimistic but I fear that our Prime Minister has underestimated the strength of public opinion in Ghana."

"I don't think that I'm going to live long enough to see any change: we must make the best of the situation as we have always done."

The two friends said goodbye and left for their own homes.

Then, one day in February 1966, at the height of the dry season, when the harmattan wind had made everything bone-dry, doors and tables cracked and warped, and you needed cream to keep your skin and lips supple, the at-first unbelievable news came through by radio; President Nkrumah had been de-stooled, deposed from office while on his way by air to China where he had flown to help to find a solution of the problems of Vietnam! Certain senior army officers, supposedly preparing a specialist combat force to overthrow the Smith regime in Southern Rhodesia, had carried out a coup d'etat and had taken over the reins of government. Everywhere throughout the land people stood amazed as the news came over the public loud-speakers from the Ghana Broadcasting Corporation later confirmed by the BBC World News. It was almost impossible to believe that the President and his CPP regime had been so easily overthrown and superseded; it was reported that there had been no bloodshed and little or no resistance to the take-over. The President would not be allowed back into the country and army officers would rule as the National Liberation Council for a period of time before handing back the functions of government to civilians. Some hours later came the news that the President would be granted asylum by Sekou Toure in Guinea where he would be granted the role of Co-President.

What would happen now? was the question on everyone's lips but there was no immediate answer, the people could only wait. They were bidden to go about their normal business and follow their usual way of life, which is what they did. They hoped, at any rate, that in the future that they would be once again free to speak their own minds, that the soldiers in the Congo would soon come home and that banned newspapers would be again free to comment on political matters. In any event, the army coup had won a breathing-space, a pause in which to assess how democracy could best work in Africa. The next few years, however, were uneasy and turbulent: the military coup was followed by others until finally Air Force Officer Jerry Rawlings, the son of a Scots father and an Ewe mother, took power and dealt severely with corruption in government. It seemed as though, at last, he could achieve permanence and economic progress. But when the two friends next met, Nana still expressed his disappointment.

"We have made some improvement but our economy remains at a very low level, we are practically bankrupt as a nation, ordinary household utensils and foodstuffs are scarce and cost more. What has happened to the cocoa industry, once our mainstay? Inflation is robbing our cedi currency of any real value and our people are chasing US dollars and English pounds! The real problem is: when does military rule give way to democratically elected civilian rule? And when that happens, how do the people control the politicians?"

Tom could only nod in agreement, and commented:

"It takes a long time for a country to find the sort of government that suits it the best. I don't want to be unduly pessimistic but it took many long years before the nations of Europe worked out a democratic system that suited them. Think of the ideal of Abraham Lincoln expressed in his speech at the end of the Civil War in the United States, that 'government of the people, by the people, for the people, shall not perish from the earth.' We are a long way, everywhere, from achieving that ideal. We can only wait and see how things turn out."

9
Chapter

❧ *A great tree is uprooted.* ❧

"The stool was in every sense greater than the man or woman who sat upon it".

R.S.Rattray, *Ashanti Law and Constitution*, page 330.

Between the queenmother, Christina Adjowa Agyeman, and her brother, Nana Oduro Panyin II, there existed a very close bond. She was two years older than he; they had grown up together, both had studied in London, he Law and she Business Methods. Afterwards she had assisted him in his practice in Kumasi and when he had been elected chief and she had become queenmother, she had worked in the office of the Gyasehene. She had won the respect of all those who came into contact with her; she had an air of good breeding; she was tall and slim like her brother, her head poised on a long, slender neck, and when you spoke with her, she gave you her full, sympathetic attention. On state occasions and in court she sat on the left side of the chief in front of the elders. She had the power to interrupt with a question in court cases and in any matter concerning the welfare of the state. Her brother and the elders valued her opinion highly.

She visited her brother every day, especially since his illness had been diagnosed, and it had become clear to her that the burden of coping with his disability had grown heavier for him and one day, as they sat together on the veranda he said:

"You know, Adjowa, my illness is growing rapidly worse; every morning I feel weak and the trembling and the attacks of dizziness grow stronger; the tablets help but for a shorter time; I don't think that I can fulfil my duties much longer."

Adjowa knew better than to contradict him. All the medical doctors had agreed that there was no known cure and the visit to the abosom had confirmed that. Throughout their lives they had spoken the absolute truth to each other and she sensed now that he had something special to discuss with her. It proved to be so.

"I have been giving the matter of my successor much thought recently because we shall need someone who will wish to continue the policies of modernisation that I and the Council have begun but at the same time would seek to preserve the best features of our traditional life. There are no brothers left in my family so it is almost certain that Owusu Kuma will be put forward by his family, and I see no alternative. He is a great traditionalist; as you know, he is by no means convinced that modern progress is all good; he fears that we shall become hybrid Europeans or Americans and lose our own African Akan identity. I can fully sympathise with his point of view but it seems to me that in the world of today there are amenities that we simply must have: a first-class educational system, clinics and hospitals, water supply and sanitation, electric light and power, tarred roads and good communications. We can have all that and still keep our own culture, the Europeans have succeeded in doing that and we should do the same. You know, Adjowa, the only man I know who fully shares my views is my friend Tom McKenzie."

She looked at him in astonishment.

"But he could never be considered as your successor surely?"

"I know that; but think of the number of stools we have, all our elders have stools and there's one stool position that's been vacant for three years since the family has no one to put forward so that I have the right to fill it at any time by nomination."

Adjowa was quick to grasp his train of thought.

"You mean the Ankobeahene? The Gyasehene has taken the responsibilty for his duties during the past three years".

"Precisely. Can you not imagine Tom McKenzie as Ankobeahene? There are good precedents for honouring him in this way: in 1930 the Asantehene gave the Basel missionary, Eugen Rapp, a stool for his specialist work in the Akan language. In 1962 the former District Commisioner in Akuapem, James Moxon, was installed in Aburi as Nana Kofi Onyaase. Both had the right to speak in Council meetings; both could speak Twi, both had a proven record of service to our people.

This is my point, my dear sister, remember what Tom McKenzie has already done for our community with the founding of the High School and think of what he brings with him through his contacts with central government. Think of the advantage of having a former Education

Department official on our Council, one who knows at first hand the tedious ways of government bureaucracy. In Council Tom could lead from behind as the saying is, he's tactful, reasonable, persuasive; think of the way he spoke with the elders about the High School project; think of the way he has recruited the staff and has welded them together in a black and white team. It would be a great pity if we lost him. As Ankobeahene he would be no longer a visitor but a permanent resident and member of Council; we would just 'adopt' him; he would become one of us. In any case, he has no family now in Britain."

"But if he gave up his job as Manager of Schools how would we pay him? We can't expect him to serve our community for nothing."

"A good question. As Ankobeahene he would be responsible for the villages of Akuraakese and Kyekyewere and he would receive a fixed sum from the Council for these duties; in addition, it is almost certain that the Education Department would make him local Education Officer for which he would be paid and Council could find ways and means of rewarding him for special services. Also on the outskirts of Kyekyewere there is an unfinished house belonging to the family; Council could negotiate with the family to finish it and to make it available for him."

"Has he any intention of taking a wife?"

"I once asked him why he hadn't married and he told me in confidence of a unsuccessful love affair; I suggested to him that he should now consider marriage. But to come back to my proposal, Adjowa: when anything happens to me, you would play an important role in choosing my successor; you would have to agree with the elders about Owusu Kuma but what do you think of my plan for Tom McKenzie?"

Nana had sensed with gratification that his sister was in favour of his plan but he wanted further to discuss with her ways and means of bringing it about. Adjowa regarded him with eyes full of deep feeling and assured him:

"I would need to ask Tom first if such a role interested him and if so it would be necessary for me to convince Kwadjo Ofori, our senior elder. I could offer full support for Owusu Kuma as your successor in return for his acceptance of Tom as Ankobeahene."

He took her hand and pressed it to his lips as a sign of his full agreement with her plan.

"There's one other important thing: you know that by our custom my widow, Amy, would be dependent on my successor for decisions about her future. Whatever custom might decree, I want you to exact a promise from Owusu Kuma to give up any claim on her, on our children or on our estate. The money that we have in the bank and our house in Kumasi is absolutely hers; it's stated in my will, not a cedi of it is stool property."

"Of course, dear brother, I shall do as you wish."

She noticed his eyelids droop and helped him to his bed; the discussion had tired him and he would soon sleep. With a last glance at him she tiptoed sadly out of the room. This sickness had taken its toll of her brother's strength but his spirit and mind were still strong and lively.

About six months later, the quietness of the High School compound was broken by frenzied shouting outside the gate. Grace awoke first and joined by Abenaa and Thelma, the three of them peered over the veranda rail into the darkness. The night watchman came running holding his hurricane lamp aloft and shouted:

"I think the Chief has gone to his village; all these strangers want us to give them protection, they say that they are afraid for their lives."

Abenaa and Grace looked at each other, both could guess what had happened. In former times when a chief passed away he had to be accompanied on his journey to the ancestors by a retinue of servants befitting his status who would serve him in the next world. Sometimes, strangers, prisoners-of-war and slaves were sacrificed. The custom had long ago been prohibited by the British but sometimes it had taken place secretly. No one ever said,' The king had died'; his passing was referred to in the phrases, 'He has gone elsewhere', or 'A great tree has been uprooted'. All this flashed through their minds. Time was critical. At that moment, Alastair and Ben appeared alongside the night watchman and Grace called out:

"Let the strangers in, then close the gate quickly and lock it."

Within a short time about twenty men were allowed inside and were permitted to sit on the floor in a storeroom and forbidden to talk or to make any noise. Ben, Alastair and the watchman stood together at the gate only minutes before a band of warriors ran up brandishing cutlasses but when they saw that the gate was guarded and locked and that there was no sign of any fugitives, they turned back towards the town.

Ben asked Grace:

"Who are our guests and what shall we do with them?"

"Give them water to drink, tell them that they are quite safe and that they should remain quiet until dawn when we shall give them something to eat. We'll find out in the morning who they are."

At first light they gave the fugitives a bowl of rice, some fried plantain and canned fish and talked with them as they ate. They were mostly northerners who had fled from the Zongo, the Moslem village on the outskirts of the town: among them were two Fulani who had trekked south with a small herd of beef cattle, three were night-soil removers employed by the Council, two were Dagomba guards at the Chief's palace who had been the first to hear the news, some were traders from across the Volta River in the Eastern Region. All were grateful to sit quietly until it was safe to leave. No attempt had been made to phone the *ahemfie* but they had been able to make contact with Tom in Kumasi who told them to stay at the school until he arrived. At midday his car drew up at the school accompanied by a police car and three officers. They related what had happened and the police interviewed the fugitives; no one had been threatened or personally hurt, they had simply fled for safety on hearing the shouting. At that point the phone rang: it was the queenmother and Tom took the receiver: "Good morning, Dr.McKenzie, I have been informed that you have arrived at the school and I am sorry to inform you that my beloved brother, our *Omanhene* and your friend has departed elsewhere. I am told that a group of strangers have taken refuge at the school and I apologise for the disturbance; it is now perfectly safe for them to return to town. I hear that the police are with you, please inform them that if they wish, they may visit the ahemfie."

"What will happen now, queenmother?"

"I cannot tell you in detail, all the formalities are in the hands of the elders. There will be the wake, the burial, the drumming and the firing of guns and last of all there will be the '*sora*' ceremony, so that after a week everything will slowly be back to normal."

"I am grateful to you, queenmother, for your telephone call. I will pass on the information to all concerned and next week I should like to call on you with my condolences."

"I should welcome that; you know how much my brother admired you and valued your friendship, he spoke to me often about you."

Tom turned to the others and told them what the queen-mother had said and what he had learned from the police:

"It seems that Nana's body was found at the foot of the steep stair which lead to his private rooms. Around him were scattered tablets from the open bottle of medicine which he still clutched in his left hand; the door at the top of the stair was open and it is thought he was overcome by an attack of dizziness, stumbled over the threshold and fell."

About two weeks later the queenmother sought an interview with the senior elder, Nana Kwadjo Ofori, and as she entered his sitting room he dismissed his servant. They exchanged traditional greetings and he repeated his condolences to her to which she replied suitably. Then the queenmother lost no time in stating her reason for meeting.

"It will be important for us to choose a suitable successor to my brother to lead us into the future."

"That is true; our world is rapidly changing and we must change with it without losing the best of our own traditions. We shall need someone, however, to further the changes that have already been made. We need an educated, dedicated man like your brother."

"That is what I should like to discuss with you. Shortly

before he departed from us my brother spoke with me about his successor and it seemed to him that Nana Owusu Kuma would be put forward by his family and that he would be the most suitable person to sustain our traditions and culture as well as accepting the need for changes. He felt, however, that the elders might accept a suggestion from him that at this time might prove beneficial to our community."

"May I say, quite frankly, that certain of the elders have expressed their feelings to me about Nana Owusu Kuma, namely, that while he would relish the duty of sustaining our traditions he might not be so interested in the problems of adapting ourselves to the impact of modern technology. You will recall that on a number of occasions he has spoken forcibly against the costs of improving our amenities and the taxation necessary to provide these things."

"Has there been mention of another candidate?"

"No, Nana, that is the problem. You did, however refer to a suggestion made by your brother before he went away."

"He spoke to me of the possibility of his friend Dr McKenzie coming to live and work among us. You know how much he has done for our community by establishing the High School; he is a man who loves our people, who speaks our language, who has won respect from every side, and who knows the ways of government. He has a Christian background but belongs to no church but he sets great store by our beliefs and traditions; a man who is at home both in the Western world and in the African world. He could advise and help us to solve all sorts of problems that beset us today."

"We all know and esteem this white man, Ena, persons of his calibre are rare. But how could we persuade him to leave a senior post in the educational world and settle down with us, even if he wished to do so? At the very least we would need money for a salary and accommodation."

"Supposing that the problems of salary and housing could be overcome, would you and the elders welcome such a man?"

"I feel sure that they would welcome him; we would benefit greatly from his advice and experience."

The queenmother paused and changed the direction of the discussion:

"Have the elders yet found a new *ankobeahene?*"

"No. The family are widely scattered and their spokesman has no one to put forward. The Gyasehene has taken over the duties for a few years now."

He looked puzzled and then as he grasped the point of the question said with a smile.

"You mean, of course, that we could offer Dr. McKenzie the stool of the Ankobeahene?"

"Yes, just that."

"What a brilliant suggestion. Was it your idea or your brother's?"

"My brother thought of it; he felt that the idea of working completely within our community would attract him. He and my brother were great friends, you know. He is not primarily motivated by monetary rewards."

"All the same, we should need to offer him an appropriate salary."

He thought for a moment and then continued:

"I feel sure that we could employ him as District

Education Officer; for that post we receive grant; in addition the Ankobeahene receives a share of the cocoa-farm rents in his district. You know that there are two large villages, Kyekyewere and Akuraakese, for which he has overall responsibility. Furthermore, there's an unfinished, well-designed house on the way to Kyekyewere which the family can't complete for lack of funds and wish to sell; I think that Council could acquire the property for staff accommodation."

Adjowa listened in delighted surprise. Opanyin Kwadjo Ofori had very shrewdly furthered her brother's suggestion. She had one final question.

"Would Dr, McKenzie, in the capacity of Ankobeahene be acceptable to Nana Owusu Kuma?"

"The proposal could be so presented to him that if he were to receive a unanimous vote from the elders and the Queen Mother to succeed to the stool, we might expect in return his support to the election of Dr. McKenzie as Ankobeahene. Give me time to mobilise the views of the elders on this matter."

"I know that my brother would be pleased that we have both agreed. I will speak with Dr.McKenzie without delay and will inform you at once of his reaction. If it is favourable we can then proceed with the elections," Adjowa concluded.

"I feel sure that I can persuade the elders of the desirability of electing Dr McKenzie as Ankobeahene and if he accepts we shall receive him as one of ourselves, he will belong to us by adoption. You can assure him of that."

She turned and clasped his hand as she thanked him and returned home. Some days later she invited Dr. McKenzie to meet her at her Kumasi house and lost no time telling him of her brother's proposal and of her talk with Nana Kwadjo Ofori. Tom was pleased and honoured by their confidence in him but he hesitated to give a definite answer and Adjowa tactfully left him alone while she prepared a meal.

It seemed to Tom that there was a kind of inevitability about the invitation; he himself had prepared the way; had he not spent years of his life learning the language, studying Akan customs and traditional religion, and working to develop educational facilities? Had he not enjoyed the friendship of Ghanaians? Had they not fully accepted him and had now invited him to take a last step of identifying himself entirely with them? He puzzled over his hestation. Why had he not at once accepted the invitation? Hadn't he felt sure for a long time that his future work lay in Ghana? To become Ankobeahene would be deeply satisfying: he would have the chance of building up the school system in the district and of deepening his friendships with the elders. Then he remembered that Kweku had once asked him why he had never married and after he had confided to him his experience with Isabel he had said: "You should take a wife now, it could make you even happier than you are." Had Kweku already at that time thought of him as one of the elders, married and maybe with children? Of course, if he were to accept the invitation, to marry would be a sensible thing to do. But at the time he had thought: Where should I go to find a partner? Who could possibly be interested in a middle-aged bachelor who seemed to have no other interest than his work? And now? Wasn't the situation just the same? And as he pondered the thought stayed in his mind with compelling force, what if in fact, there was someone who had a definite interest in him and his work? And in a flash, he realised without a shadow of doubt, that the 'someone' was Thelma Morrow! Right from the time of her arrival in Ghana they had got on well together: he had learned to value her views on school matters, her contributions at staff meetings, her success with the children in the classroom, her positive attitude and good humour, her love for Africa. Had she not made it clear to him that she enjoyed his company? How stupid he had been not to see it! Perhaps all this time she had been waiting and hoping that their relationship might reach a deeper level! And always he had continued to keep himself isolated within the self-assured solitude that he had adopted after his affair with Isabel had come to an end. He knew now, without any doubt at all, that he was in love with Thelma and for that reason he had hesitated to accept the invitation at once! If Thelma would marry him he would say 'Yes' immediately to the queenmother!

Adjowa called him in to the lunch that she had prepared and when they sat at the table she looked at him expectantly.

"I am greatly honoured by the invitation to become Ankobeahene, your brother was my best friend and it would be a challenge to me to try to support his ideas for the future of the town and district. May I say that I should like to accept the invitation but there is an important personal matter that I must clear up first. Can you and the elders wait until the week-end for my final answer? I will call at the ahemfie on Saturday to give you my firm decision."

Adjowa smiled contentedly; her mission had not failed, he had said that he would like to accept and it was only right and proper that he should have more time. When lunch was over they shook hands cordially and Tom took his leave but as soon as he reached home he began a furious debate with himself: his problem was a totally different one now! How, at extremely short notice, do you ask an attractive woman, at least twenty years younger than yourself, to marry you when your relationship has never been intimate and no word of love has ever been spoken? Tom was full of self-recrimination, accusing himself of lack of intelligence, to think that because of Isabel he should remain a bachelor all his days! Was it not equally true to believe that fate had sent Thelma into his life? But why had he never before thought of Thelma in this way? In fact, he had been so preoccupied with his work that he had only regarded her as a first-class recruit to the school staff. In any case she was not of his generation; he was the employer, the elderly bachelor who seemingly preferred to live alone! He had been alone with Thelma on very few occasions but their discussions had always been friendly and helpful; he had an impression that she had wanted specially to help him to start the High School because she was full of suggestions for organisation and curriculum but it had never occurred to him that she was also interested in him as a person. He'd always felt at ease with her: like him she had an affection for Africa and things African. He was older than she but was that so important? There were many things that he didn't know about her and which she didn't know about him but wasn't that normal when you fell in love with someone? His thoughts came back again and again to the overwhelming conviction that he had fallen in love with her without being consciously aware of the fact; he felt towards her in the same way that he had experienced towards Isabel, a feeling that he had never thought could be repeated. The offer of the Ankobea stool had worked like a catalyst in bringing him to the realisation of his love for her. He must see her and talk with her as soon as possible, but how could he arrange a meeting so that he could talk with Thelma alone without arousing the curiosity of others? Finally Tom thought of a simple plan: Thelma helped at the clinic on Thursday afternoons and as the clinic was relatively isolated at the end of town he could call in there, so to speak, by chance.

His heart was pounding as he drew near the whitewashed building with its green-painted roof; yes, she was there, the bicycle that she and Grace shared was leaning against the rear wall. He parked his Land Rover on the roadside and as he approached he could see that the nurse, Catharina, was giving a talk to a group of women in the courtyard. Thelma was alone in the storeroom and glanced up in surprise as he knocked on the open door and walked in. He heard himself saying:

"Can I see you alone for a few minutes?"

She offered him the only chair and seated herself on an unpacked crate. She was faintly alarmed because she had sensed an urgency in his tone and a frown of anxiety crossed her forehead.

"Is there bad news about my family or about the school?"

"No, Thelma, nothing like that but there is an urgent personal matter that I want to discuss with you—."

His voice tailed off and he paused to recover his calmness of mind.

"There is something that I have to tell you, Thelma, I've been asked by the Queen Mother to consider giving up my job in Kumasi and accepting the position of *Ankobeahene* here in Bechemantia. He is one of the elders who is most concerned with the organisation of local matters in the town and district; it is likely that I would become the District Education Officer too and help the Council in other general ways. It would be something that I should very much like to do but it would mean living here and becoming closely identified with the local community. Before I could come to a firm decision to accept it became clear to me that I had first to discuss the matter with you."

"But why with me?" Thelma queried sharply.

"Because when I was thinking over the offer I realised that I was in love with you, that in the future I wanted to share my life with you, that I wanted to marry you. You see, Thelma, if you married me you would be the wife of one of the elders in a small town in Brong Ahafo which would then be your home in the future. Of course, if you thought that you could never return my love and marry me, the matter would end there."

Like all women, on these occasions when they have to make a decision affecting their lives in the deepest possible way, Thelma thought with lightning speed. She knew instinctively that Tom was a man she could trust absolutely; from the beginning of her acquaintance with him she had been sure that he was the sort of man that she could live and work with. She had come to admire and respect him and even to hope that one day their friendship might move on to a deeper level, but as time had passed this hope had dimmed. Now, out of the blue, she was required to make an instant decision; a declaration of love has an air of finality about it, it's a Yes/No, once-for-all avowal which demands a reaction. Thelma delayed giving a direct answer so as to gain a bit more time.

"Tom, listen. When a man tells a woman that he loves her, the way he earns a living isn't top priority; of course, it's part of the total package but normally what she is most concerned about is what they have in common, like interests, ideas, way of life, likes and dislikes; whether he'll be good to live with, whether he's likely to be a good father of children and be a good homemaker, that sort of thing."

She was smiling as she spoke and Tom took her smile to be an encouragement to say more. How attractive she was! Why hadn't he been aware of it before? How stupid he had been not to have let her see that he found her charming! A note of pleading entered his voice as he continued and her eyes never left his face.

"When I met you for the first time at Accra Airport and we talked that day and the following day during the drive to Kumasi, I felt so much at ease with you. When I shared my plans for the school with you and I told you about the way that education had developed in Ghana you showed such a constructive interest that I felt deeply fortunate that you would be joining the staff. Later you made valuable contributions at staff meetings so that Kwesi and Grace came to rely on you; I felt that the school project would be greatly strengthened because of your experience and the skill of your teaching. We had so much in common in working for the school; you fitted in well with everbody, you began learning the language, you volunteered for work at the clinic and I knew then that you had the same interest in teaching in Ghana as I had. Why didn't I try then to make our friendship closer? I was often so busy but also I had been a bachelor for so long that I felt that I didn't really belong to your generation; more than that, I was in a kind of official position to the school and towards the Peace Corps so that it wasn't easy for me to bridge the gap completely, paticularly if I began to show a preference for the company of one of school's female staff. I could go on, Thelma, but it was only when the invitation was made did I truly realise that it was much more than admiration for you that I had, it was love. Love isn't something that I know much about; I got to know a girl at university when I was a student and we intended to marry but my father and her parents prevented it. I left home permanently aferwards and buried myself in my work. I never thought that someone like you would come into my life. I love you, Thelma and I want you to be my wife."

She turned to him and took both his hands in hers.

"Oh, Tom McKenzie, you're the kindest, honestest, modestest man I've ever known. We all admire you but I am your biggest fan. For quite some time I have secretly hoped that one day you would come out of your shell and speak to me as you have done now; it's the wonderfullest day of my life! Yes, yes, yes! I love you too, I will marry you and live with you and help you with your work all I can right here in this town."

Their faces came together and their lips met for quite a while until Thelma whispered softly in his ear.

"We have been seen; Catharina looked in and hastily drew back."

Tom murmured in reply:

"It's OK. I'll come up again on Friday week and announce our engagement so that everybody knows."

"Tom, before you go, I have just three quick questions: when we are living together, can we travel to the US occasionally to visit with my family? Maybe you could show me Scotland too, and could we live in a house somewhere with views over the forest?"

Tom responded joyfully.

"Yes to all three questions! There are some things I don't yet know the answers to, like salary. The Ankobeahene has two villages to look after, one is called Kyekyewere, that means 'Comfort' in English; near that village is a half-built modern house overlooking a wide valley and forested hills which I think that the Council would get ready for us."

He jumped into his Land Rover and drove off with a wave of his hand. During the drive back to Kumasi all sorts of delightful images flashed across the screen of his mind, pictures of an exciting future with Thelma as his partner. What a difference an hour can make to transform his entire life!

On his return he phoned his acceptance to the queen-mother who assured him that the elders' tacit agreement had been given so that when he visited the school the following weekend he saw at once that the news was known. He was met by Grace and Kwesi and led into the staff room to meet the beaming faces and warm handshakes of all of them. Kwesi took the chair and said with a smile:

"We have only one item on the agenda for today's meeting and that is: Announcement by Dr McKenzie, General Manager of Schools."

Tom stood up and looked around; pupils were clustered around outside looking in through the windows, there were bottles and glasses on a side table, a huge wreath of flowers hung above the notice board, but above all, there was a sudden deep silence and an atmosphere of intense expectancy. It was clear to him that his two pieces of news were already known but they wanted to hear the confirmation from his own lips.

"Headmaster and colleagues, I want you to know that the queenmother and the elders have unanimously invited me to become the *Ankobeahene* of Bechemantia and that I have accepted. For the school it means that whenever you need help and advice I shall always be at your disposal and not have to drive from Kumasi."

He paused there, and as the applause rippled round the room he looked directly at Thelma who nodded imperceptably as if to say, 'they've heard about our meeting at the clinic, you can tell them now.'

"I have one other piece of news which will be of interest to you all: Miss Thelma Morrow and I have become engaged and intend to marry."

This time the applause was loud and prolonged. He beckoned to Thelma to come forward. He had brought one of his mother's rings with him, took her left hand and slipped it on the third finger; for an anxious moment it hesitated before going over the knuckle, and then she held up her face for his kiss. It couldn't have been better done if they had rehearsed it.The staff crowded round to congratulate them, everyone was elated at the news that Thelma would marry Dr.McKenzie.

Later in the Council there was the same warmth and affection shown towards them and Thelma and Tom both felt that the seal had been given to both their decisions. Last of all, on that memorable day, as they sat together in Thelma's room they exchanged the confidences that lovers indulge in, each wanting to tell the other about their home and family, as well as their life before they had met. Tom spoke of Isabel and of his unhappy relationship with his father and the reason for his decision to leave home; Thelma listened so pensively and silently that Tom asked:

"Is anything the matter?"

Thelma was thinking furiously of her two encounters

with Wayne and Duncan: she wanted to be as frank with Tom as he had been with her, yet there was a certain risk that he might gain a false impression of her nature. What was certain, was that her coming to Ghana had proved to have been the right decision. She had become utterly absorbed in her work and had come to understand herself, Tom had sought her out and she had accepted him. What they had known then of each other had been enough.

"Yes, there is something that you should know about me, when I was in my final year at high school I had a relationship with my Science teacher. He was 60 years old, a widower who lived alone not far from our farm and who gave me a lift to school and back every day. Then at university I had an affair with a fellow student and we planned to marry but I broke off the engagement because our views of the civil rights struggle of the blacks in the USA were completely different. It was then that I volunteered for work in Ghana because my great-grandmother was born there and also because I wanted time to sort my life out."

She paused and Tom said:

"I suppose that most attractive girls these days have similar experiences, are you suggesting that these episodes have somehow spoilt you for marriage?"

"No, not at all, but after what has happened between us, I wanted you to know that I wasn't in love with either of them. From the day that I first met you I felt at home with you and the longer I got to know you - your ideas for the school, your love for this land and its people, your dedication – all made me realise that you had found your real vocation and it inspired me to want to do the same. My two affairs taught me that much that when I fell in love the lasting bond would be a a sharing of minds and a mutual striving after something that we both wanted to achieve."

Tom broke in abruptly to reassure her.

"Listen, Thelma, we are both at the threshold of a marvellous new relationship for us both here and now. Attachments that we have had in the past have taught us something but what is important for both of us from now on is to build on what we have in common, what we aready share. Chance has brought you and me finally together; you know, at one time I thought that you had a special interest in Ben."

"Well, we became good friends right away: we had VSO and Peace Corps in common, we both had Ghanaian roots and English was our mother tongue. He told me what had happened to him in Agokro which really interested me, the notion that as an 'ababio' he had a special task to fulfil. But we never became close friends, he was more interested in what was going on around him than in his own thoughts and feelings, whereas I am much more concerned with motivations and attitudes, Now that he is in love with Grace, she is slowly getting him to express his thoughts and emotions and he is entering a new world! She's the ideal person for him. Did you know that they are both crazy about classical music and that listening to Mozart brought them together?"

"And working in Ghana in Brong Ahafo High School has brought us together!"

They laughed happily and embraced. It had been a long and memorable day!

The Celebration of the annual Festival

Afe anno ahyia, yebetwe odwira; asamanfo, omma bone biara mma, na afe foforo nto yen bokoo. (A full year has passed, we are about to celebrate the rites of the odwira; do not permit any evil at all to come upon us and let the new year meet us peacefully). From the prayer at the beginning of the festival.

R. S. Rattray, *Religion and Art in Ashanti*, Oxford 1927, p.128.

In almost every large town in Ghana an annual festival takes place when everyone who has links with the town and district returns for the celebration. In Akuapem and Akyem it is called Odwira, but in some other areas they have other names like Akwasidae (Ashanti), Ohum (Guan), Homowo (Ga-Adangbe), Fetu Afahye (Cape Coast) and Bakatue (Elmina). But whatever the name, the occasion is a time of renewal and rejoicing, a time to revisit your birthplace, a time to meet former classmates and colleagues and a time of reunion for scattered members of extended families. But the festival has also deeply-ingrained associations: ancestors who have passed away are remembered, the ancestral stools are purified, the stool of the present chief is paraded and the spectators symbolically renew their loyalty to it, the newly-harvested yam can now be eaten and a new year begun. Everything is a reminder of the on-going life of the community, a reminder of the spiritual world of the ancestors whose favour is sought for another year. In all these aspects the festival enshrines the identity, the unity and the continuity of the people. It lasts a few days, sometimes longer, because many traditional rituals have to be performed and there is usually a durbar and procession of chiefs and notables. During these days the towns are crowded and the streets are thronged with citizens, day and night.

Tom McKenzie, the new Ankobeahene, was standing alone at the place of assembly for the festival procession; he was dressed in traditional Ghanaian male dress, wearing a richly-woven silk ntama with the right shoulder uncovered, a decorated headband, a silver chain around his neck and Akan-style sandals on his feet. As his new colleagues arrived, the Okyeame, the Gyase hene, the Kontirehene. the *Abrofohene* and others, all town councillors, they greeted him warmly. Tom felt glad to be there among them, it was the outward and visible sign that he had been accepted as one of themselves. A small hand tugged at his ntama, it was that of a young boy, smartly-dressed, who sought his attention, and as Tom turned he looked directly into Tom's face with that unwavering, trustful, steady gaze that young children possess, smiled and said:

"I am ordered by my mother to give this to you personally, and only to you."

He extended his right hand in which he held a small cardboard box wrapped in gold-coloured paper which Tom accepted. He carefully opened the box, took out a visiting card on which was written:

Please accept this ring from my late brother. He wanted you to have it and to wear it in his memory as his very close friend. Dear Tom, you are one of us now and I am so glad.

Your sincere friend,
Christina Adjowa Agyeman.

He could feel the tears rising in his eyes as he saw, inside the box, nestling on a pad of purple velvet, the lustrous gold ring which Nana Oduro had always worn. The eyes of all his colleagues were now turned on him with eager interest. Tom took out the ring and held it up for all to see before placing it on the forefinger of his right hand; he then gravely shook the boy's hand and murmured his thanks. Reaching into his shirt breast pocket he took out the silver pencil that he always carried. It was a present from his aunt on his graduation and bore his initials; he handed it to the boy and said:

"This pencil belonged to me, now it is yours. Tell your mother that I am most grateful for the kind gift of her brother's ring, I shall wear it always. I shall write to her."

The boy turned away politely and went back home. Tom's colleagues nodded their approval of his return gift, it was a traditional gesture that they much appreciated.

An announcement was made that the procession was ready to move off and that the elders would walk behind the chief's palanquin which was accompanied by the sword-bearers, the horn-blowers, and directly in front of the elders by the two fontomfrom drums on the heads of two carriers. They didn't march, the parade moved too slowly for that. On each side of the road the cheering crowds stood three and four deep to get a glimpse of the new chief and the new queenmother as well as all the elders in their finery. Occasionally a spectator would dart out to shout a personal greeting to Nana or to the queenmother to be rewarded by a smile and a wave of the hand. Sometimes one of the uniformly-dressed singing bands would break into song in the unique way Akans have, when one of their number leads off with a recitative of praise or thanks to be joined by the combined group in their own special harmony producing a deep wave of sound that strikes deep into the heart and mind. At intervals the hornblowers gave a sample of their special expertise which the drummers would follow with a torrent of rapid, staccato bursts of sound, and meanwhile, all along the route impromptu dancers found space to express in their steps and bodily movements their joy at being part of the occasion.

All this while, Tom was thinking of his decision to commit himself to live and work among these kind folk who had welcomed him and adopted him as one of themselves. He really had a home now – in Ghana. And along with that commitment had come Thelma, who was now sharing it with him. How discerning Nana and his sister had been, to see that the offer of the appointment as Ankobeahene and of Education Officer with the Council would act as a catalyst which would solve the problem of the seeming aloofness of his bachelor state! Had they intuitively sensed that Thelma would be the right wife for him? He had always hesitated to use the words 'happy' and 'happiness' because of his experience with Isabel and also because people tended to assume that marriage automatically brought 'happiness'. He had always preferred to use the word 'contentment' to describe the married state, a result of mutual interest, respect, affection, tolerance, trust and the ability to live and work together. Maybe all these things added up to love. In this respect Thelma had re-made and re-routed his life and he could truly say that his cup of contentment was full!

He continued musing over the three possible projects that he would like to submit to Council: there was the small dam that could be built in the narrow gorge in the hill to the west of the town; the stream had never failed in living memory even in the driest weather and there were enough stones nearby to build a dam ten metres wide and five metres high that would create a lake that would hold a few thousand cubic metres of fresh drinking water! This water could be piped to two villages as well as to an inexhaustible well in the town! All at relative small cost. Of course the Akosombo Dam promised electric power and a water supply for all Ghana but in any case to have their own extra drinking water source would be an advantage. His second proposal was to improve the facilities at the clinic; again a matter of funds; the third plan was a good library for the High School. He was sunk in deep thought about the financing of these schemes when among the spectators he saw the High School group. It seemed that all the school staff were there led by the Headmaster, Kwesi Akuffo, and Tom soon made out Thelma, Grace and Ben, Alastair and Abenaa with her mother and a man whom he didn't recognise. Cameras were pointing at him and raised hands were clapping with enthusiasm; he waved to them and gave them all a broad smile. How well all the staff, African and European, had worked together as a team was remarkable and was a tribute to the leadership of Kwesi, Grace and Thelma.

As the procession moved on Kwesi resumed his role as guide. He was always in his element explaining Ghana traditions and customs and on this occasion there was much to explain.

"The annual festival celebration brings together the yam harvest, a new year, remembrance of our ancestors, the honouring of our chiefs past and present, loyalty to the stool, hope for the future of our town, and thanksgiving for our continuing life together. The entire community joins in, whatever your religion or beliefs. Everything you see or hear has a special significance, just ask me."

Alastair wanted to know why the drums were often referred to by Europeans as 'talking drums', was it some kind of telegraph?

The drums 'speak', Kwesi made clear, because they beat out well-known proverbs or popular sayings or verses which most people know; in addition the drummers on festival occasions sound out praise names of the chiefs or make references to events in our past history. Each syllable is beaten out with its proper rhythm and tone and then all the drums join in with a number of repetitions. People can recognise the different phrases, but if they can't, the drummers know. So if, for example, you heard the drums at a distance, you would know which chief it was. Every chief has his 'strong' name which identifies him. The hornblowers also have their repertoire to herald the presence of a particular chief.

Someone else asked why the staff of office of the okyeame was topped by a gilded carving of a snail being carried by a tortoise.

"It's a sign of harmony and peace," explained Kwesi. "If there's any trouble, these creatures simply withdraw into their shells, they don't quarrel and fight. But we also have two other meanings associated with the snail and the tortoise: If somebody offers you a lift, you don't say, I'll walk. The second saying is: If the snail and the tortoise were the only creatures in the forest, the hunter's gun would never be fired! You see, Akans have a proverb for everything!"

"Do the umbrellas have a special significance?"

"Yes, they do. In Ghana, the large, coloured umbrellas or sunshades announce the presence of someone important. There's a proverb that's applicable: *Onyame nhu ohene apampam;* Onyame should not see the crown of a chief's head! Meaning that the sunshade is a shield from the envy of Nyame! When the umbrella is raised up and down so that the fringe and the flounces flutter the umbrella is 'dancing' in tribute. The VIP under the umbrella is, of course, given shade and coolness."

"Why is the chief's stool and the gilded, studded chairs carried on the head upside down?" was another question.

"You all know that every important person in the community possesses their own stool carved in the tradi- tional way because the stool is a very personal symbol of authority. The stool of the chief is the most important stool; the chief is the first in rank, the highest representative of the entire community; he is the link between the living and the ancestors. So the chief's stool is not just a ceremonial seat but a shrine and when he passes away it is blackened and placed in the stoolhouse, no one else may ever sit on it, not even invisible spirits. It is carried today as the supreme traditional embodiment of authority in the community, and upside down because no one other than the chief may sit on it. The chairs, studded with brass-headed nails, are always made on a solid wooden frame with a leather seat and back; they are symbols of stability. You will see them in the ahemfie where they are offered to visitors on ceremonial occasions and from time to time, like now, they are shown to the public."

On their way back they saw again the palanquins of the chief and of the queenmother halted in front of the ahemfie. Around that of the chief stood his personal bodyguard with their ceremonial swords with gold hilts. The palanquin was being lowered to the ground by eight strong men as Nana and his 'soul' descended; the chief looked resplendent in his regalia: he wore a rich kente cloth patterned in gold, green and red, a blue headband studded with gold, carved segments encircled his forehead while his fingers and forearms were adorned with gold rings, bracelets and amulets. His 'soul', a young boy who never left his side on ceremonial occasions, attended him and was wearing a cap ornamented with gilded goat's horns, around his neck was a string of beads and on his body were finger smears of white clay. As the queenmother stepped out from her palanquin she was attended by a women's group in matching dress, swaying as they sang in her praise. It formed a wonderful climax to their visit to the festival procession.

Before he finally left them Kwesi said:

"There is still part of the total celebration to take place tomorrow, a purification ritual when the blackened stools of former chiefs in the stoolhouse are sprinkled with pure water and a portion of new yam is offered to each one of them, and the Chief will petition the ancestors with phrases like:

"The edges of the years have met, I take new yams and give you that you may eat. Give life to me, give life to all my people; when women go to cultivate the farms, grant that food comes forth in abundance. Do not allow any illness to come."

"It's a prayer for prosperity for everybody and it sums up the festival: our link with the ancestors is still firm, that's what holds us all together. It means a lot to us, it's really something to feel good about, so it's a very special time. Goodbye now!" He smiled and waved to his colleagues who had been listening to him and they waved back. What they had witnessed had not been something staged for tourists but was a living and vivid expression of ongoing Akan life!

Later that day, Thelma and Tom were sitting together on the terrace of their home in Kyekyewere, as they had now become accustomed to do at sundown, watching the last glow of twilight fade from the sky. On the path below them a family group was making its late way home from their plantation in the forest, one of them was leading the way by the flickering light of a hurricane lamp, the others were headloading vegetables, plantain, yams, cassava and firewood. Only the shrill chirping of a forest cicada broke the silence. Tom said: "After such a tremendous day of rejoicing, with its drumming and dancing, its singing and its hubbub of voices, I'm glad to enjoy the silence that the end of the day brings. Did you ever read the 'Elegy' poem by the English writer Gray, Thelma? He composed it overlooking the churchyard where his ancestors lay buried. At sunset two lines from the opening verse always come into my mind:

    'The ploughman homeward plods his weary way,

    And leaves the world to darkness and to me.'

"You see, Thelma, the darkness belongs to me, to us, as well as the daylight; that's when we let the night give us time to absorb and assess all the impresions and experiences of the day. But Gray was thinking of something else: he was thinking of all the village folk who lie in their graves, who lived obscure lives, who never did anything special, who are not remembered for any outstanding achievement, who just worked and grew older and died. What might these obscure ancestors have achieved in their lives if only thngs had been different? I mean, if they had had the chance to go to grammar school and university they might have lived quite varied lives and become famous in some particular sphere. Gray takes comfort in the idea that just doing humble but necessary tasks all your life is in itself a kind of achievement: he writes,

    'Full many a flower is born to blush unseen!'

"You know, what we plan to do together here is ordinary and undistinguished.Before you tell me what you think Thelma, let's have a gin and tonic to celebrate today!"

11

Chapter

ᵈᔆ *Thelma and Tom visit the USA* ᔆᵈ

Odomankoma boo owuo na owuo kum no. (The Creator created
death and death killed him).
Twi Proverbs, C.A.Akrofi, Macmillan, London, 1958.

Since his installation as Ankobeahene, Thelma and Tom
had been living together and had taken over the unfinished house on the outskirts of the village of
Kyekyewere. Council workers had quickly got a roof on and
brought piped water and electricity to the site while carpenters and painters had been busy. The pair had exchanged
vows as man and wife before the Council Clerk so that
Thelma now had the name McKenzie but she had insisted
on keeping the name Morrow because it was her special link
with Ghana and great-grandmother Afua! As soon as his
duties were finished in Kumasi they had moved in. Thelma's
parents had flown over for the wedding and the previous
New Year they had visited Scotland. Their life together was
rich and full, only the news from the USA distressed them.

Since 1957 when the attempts to achieve mixed schools

had begun, racial tensions between whites and blacks had grown. Local Councils in some southern states had adopted delaying tactics to prevent the enrolment of black children in so-called 'white' schools.The Baptist pastor, Martin Luther King, had formed the Southern Christian Leadership Conference to support the protest movements and together with the National Association for the Advancement of Coloured People he organised 'sit-ins' and boycotts. As leader of the Civil Rights Movement, Martin Luther King was arrested and imprisoned but was released on the direct order of President J.F. Kennedy who later ordered federal troops and the National Guard to protect black demonstrators and who in June 1963 presented a wide-ranging Civil Rights Bill to Congress. The Bill was not passed and in November of that year the President was assassinated in Dallas, Texas. Racial attitudes hardened and although the next President, Lyndon Johnson, suceeded in getting the Civil Rights Bill approved there remained many areas where whites would not co-operate. The secret society, the Klu Klux Klan, still terrorised and lynched blacks so that the disappointment, frustration and anger of the blacks grew. Many lost faith in the method of peaceful protest advocated by Martin Luther King and militant black groups emerged like the Black Panthers with black Moslem support, who argued for revolution by force and even for separate black states. Demonstrations often developed into race riots, the word 'confrontation' emerged as a rallying cry and violence grew. In August 1965, in the suburb of Watts, Los Angeles a mass protest ended in fighting in the streets where 24 people were killed and over 1000 injured. In the following year there were similar riots in Chicago, Cleveland, New York, Detroit and in other large cities. And when in April 1968, Martin Luther King was shot and killed by a white man, it seemed to many blacks that all hope was lost. A special commission set up by President Johnson criticised both black militancy and police aggressiveness but concluded by declaring that the chief cause was white racism. The demonstrations continued in a somewhat quieter atmosphere but it was always possible for violence to break out and a solution to the problem seemed as far away as ever.

Tom used often to describe racial discrimination, slavery, persecutions, wars and genocides as man-made catastrophes which can never be reversed or erased from world history; they are permanently recorded; you can't go back to a time before they happened, they can't be atoned for and you can't bring innocent people back to life. He would say, "Somewhere in the world, at a particular time and place, a man-made catastrophe was started and its effects have persisted until today and will still persist. Natural catastrophes, like earthquakes, volcanic eruptions, floods, fires, and the like, can cause great suffering and death, but they come to an end; man-made catastrophes go on for ever, they affect the good and the bad, the innocent and the guilty alike with their corrosion. Think of the suffering, misery and death that slavery and race hatred have caused: during the Civil War in the United States; half a million men were killed or died, and even a hundred years after the end of the war and after the declaration that 'all men are created equal', civil rights for the blacks are as far away as ever. It seems that President Kennedy, Martin Luther King, Malcom X and many others died in vain."

And whenever he spoke in this way, Thelma would ask him: "What then can we do?"

Tom would answer: "We do what little we can to minimise these effects mainly by showing which side we are on."

And that was why in 1970 they decided to visit the USA during the long break before the new academic year at the High School. They visited Thelma's parents and made contact with Pauline Jones in Washington. From some of her former colleagues at the school in Baltimore came an invitation to them both to take part in a peaceful demonstration for civil rights there, organised mainly by the staffs of the city and district schools, as well as by some of the churches. The groups assembled at the City Centre: their route lay along Charles Street and Pratt Street to the Harbour and had been approved by the authorites; police stood on both sides of the road at regular intervals in front of the spectators on the sidewalk and a detachment of federal troops waited in reserve. Before setting out, the groups taking part in the demonstration joined hands to sing the song that had become the special hymn of the civil rights movement:

'We shall overcome, we shall overcome,

We shall overcome some day;

Oh, deep in my heart I do believe

We shall overcome some day.'

And then they were led off down the main street by a small jazz group to the strains of 'When the saints go marching in'. At the Harbour, where many spectators had gathered,they stopped to sing the chorus of 'Black and Blue' made famous by Louis Armstrong and which was the first time a popular song had taken race relations as its subject.

Hundreds of voices were raised in a great swell of sound:

> What did I do to be so black and blue
> They laugh at you and scorn you too.
> I'm white inside but that don't help my case;
> Because I can't hide what is in my face.
> What did I do to be so black and blue?
> How will it end? Ain't got a friend!
> My only sin is in my skin.
> What did I do to be so black and blue?

As the last words of the melody died away , a deep bass voice recited the moving phrases of Martin Luther King which begin: "I have a dream" – and then like the crack of a whiplash a gun shot shattered the deep silence of the crowd. It was never discovered who fired the shot, a militant or a trigger-happy policeman, or what had happened to account for the shot but on the instant the densely-packed mass of spectators on the sidewalks and the demonstrators in the roadway were running away in panic from the direction of the shot. There was a virtual avalanche of human beings with only one thought, to flee to a place of safety: the pressure of bodies was so great that it was impossible to do anything else than allow oneself to be carried along. The police were quite powerless and they themselves became part of the headlong stampede. Thelma and Tom linked arms and kept together but were forced inexorably forwards. Suddenly, in front of them, a young girl lost her footing and fell to the ground and was being trampled on. Tom shouted to Thelma:

"I must help her. Stay by the railings at the harbour till I come back, you will be safe there."

By sheer force he held his ground long enough to pick up the girl and hold her aloft and then he was lost to her view. Thelma was impelled further forwards until as the road widened she was able to fight her way to the left and clung to the railings until the mad rush of frightened people had abated. An hour must have passed and there was no sign of Tom but still she waited, her anxiety increasing. At last, when the crowd had almost dispersed, a policeman came to her and asked:

"Is your name McKenzie?"

Thelma nodded dumbly.

"Your husband was found unconscious holding a young girl in his arms on the other side of the road; he has been severely injured by a car that had driven onto the sidewalk trying to make a way through, the driver did not stop. Your husband and the girl have been taken to the intensive care unit in Mercy Hospital and I am instructed to take you there. My mate is waiting in the car for us". He took her arm gently and escorted her to the waiting police car. As soon as Thelma saw the face of the surgeon at the hospital she knew that he had bad news for her.

"I am deeply sorry, Madam, to have to tell you that your husband died a few minutes ago. We did everything possible to save him but the injuries to his head were too severe. The little girl has survived, he had clasped her close to him and she was shielded by his body."

For a moment Thelma gazed at him in unbelief, then her whole personality seemed to freeze as the overwhelming sense of the loss of Tom stunned her. The surgeon led her to a chair and gave her a sedative and he and the policemen, one black, one white, waited sympathetically as her grief gave way to tears. Death had come without warning like the pistol shot that had caused the panic stampede, and Tom had given his life to save a black girl whom he didn't know, and

now her world had come to an end. At last she spoke
through her tears to them:

"I suppose there are things you have to know; my
husband was British and I was born and bred in the USA.
Please look into my handbag for my passport and my
parents' address."

"Your huband's passport has been given to the police
already," said the surgeon," may they take down the details?
We shall phone your parents at once."

Thelma nodded assent to the doctor who led her to a
reclining chair, gave her a tablet and covered her with a
blanket. Then slowly as the sedative took effect, she felt
herself slipping away into a kind of numbness which
softened the piercing hurt of her grief and finally she slept.
Some hours later her parents arrived to take her home where
for days she sat quite still or lay in bed, hardly eating or sleeping or speaking, simply thinking, suffering and weeping.
Their life together had been so short: sometimes she felt
cheated and resentful, sometimes frustrated and bemoaning,
why should this tragedy have happened to her? Sudden death
gives you no time to prepare yourself for the loss of a loved
one, the awful finality of it is absolute and overwhelming.
Her parents wisely left her alone with her grief but would
often sit with her without speaking and their silent presence
had strengthened her. The sheer force of the emotional
shock began to lessen in intensity and she could start to think
again, even to think about the future. She had a formula now:
What would Tom advise her to do? She remembered so
clearly that when they had heard of the murder of Martin
Luther King he had used the word 'catastrophe' to describe
it; his death was irreversible but the cause for which he died

must be carried through. He had sacrificed his life but the burden that he was bearing must now be borne by others. So Tom had thought and had acted accordingly. How Tom had loved words! He used to say that God created by words, He carried out His purpose by words. There are words that exactly describe thoughts, ideas and feelings, words that enshrine the deepest meanings. How much she had learned from him since she had come to Ghana! How patient he had been with her questions! How he always saw the best in everyone and welcomed their contribution! How he respected everyone who came into contact with him, black or white! Above all, how he accepted life as it was and people as they were! With him she had learned to be free from the endless preoccupation with herself and had learned to lose herself in her work and in her relationships with others. Her greatest regret now was that she had not told him that she was almost certainly pregnant and had waited for a favourable occasion in America to give him the news. How glad he would have been! She pictured him in her mind holding his child in his arms with wonder and delight and as she did so the pain of his death swept over her again; why, oh why, when you have given your heart and soul to someone is their loss so devastating?

Her mother came quietly into her room and as usual sat with her without speaking but after an interval she broke the silence because she sensed that her daughter had so far recovered her calmness of mind:

"Have you decided what you will do, Thelma?"

"Yes, mother, I know now what I shall do. I'm sure that it is what Tom would have wanted me to do: I'm going back to Ghana and his child will be born there. I shall go on with my work at the High School and at the clinic and I shall finish the house and live there. I shall take Tom's ashes back with me and I shall ask permission to bury them in the school grounds."

Her tears were streaming down her cheeks now but she blinked them back and continued:

"You see, mother, he has no family to mourn him and honour him except me and my child but we shall have a memorial service so that all his Ghanaian friends can come; they will make sure that he is properly mourned and sent to his ancestors in true Akan style. They loved him too, he was adopted by them and he felt privileged to belong to them. I have been looking through Tom's letters that he had with him and there was one that the late chief had written to him not long before he died. He had been writing about his illness which he bore bravely for years and he had written: 'What can't be avoided, must be welcomed,' and Tom had underlined his words. Tom lived in that spirit, too, and you understand, don't you, that I have to do the same? That's what I want to do now. Will you and Dad help me?"

"Of course we understand, and we shall help you," they replied.

Mother and daughter held each other close and both wept, but this time the tears were full of comfort and healing. That evening Thelma wrote a letter to the chief and to the Council to ask if they could agree to her request to bury Tom's ashes in the grounds of the school. It was the first step in her recovery.

During the long vacation when the school was closed and everyone had dispersed, senior staff took turns to join the office staff to attend to urgent messages so that it was Grace who was the first to hear the terrible news: at midday the phone gave out its strident ring and she took up the receiver. It was a man's voice speaking English, a little faint but clear.

"My name is Morrow, I am Thelma Morrow's father speaking from America; to whom am I speaking?"

"I am Grace Amponsa, the Deputy Headmistress, can I take a message?"

"Yes. I am deeply grieved to tell you that Thelma's husband Tom was killed in an accident yesterday in Baltimore. He and Thelma had taken part in a demonstration procession of black people as part of the national civil rights campaign; some of Thelma's former colleagues had invited them. The demonstration was almost over when a shot was fired and suddenly there was chaos as thousands of people started running for safety and anyone who fell down was in danger of being trampled upon. Tom turned to rescue a young black girl who had fallen and he managed to reach the sidewalk but then they were hit by a car. Thelma was taken by the police to the hospital but Tom had died of head injuries. The girl recovered. Thelma is with us at home deeply shocked. I will phone again in a few days when Thelma has recovered a bit and has decided what she will do."

"We are very, very sorry to hear the news, Mr Morrow. Please give our condolences to Thelma."

They said goodbye and Grace replaced the receiver and leaned back in her chair numbed by shock and grief and when Ben came into the office a short time later and saw her tears she pointed to the telephone and said:

"I've just had the most frightful news from Thelma's father in America, Tom has been killed in a civil rights demo. in Baltimore."

Grace gave him the details and they sat silent for a while as though stunned. It was Ben who spoke first.

"We have to phone Kwesi at his home, and then the ahemfie. The Education Office will have to know officially as well as the chief and the elders." Kwesi told them that he would come immediately; they should wait until he arrived and as they waited Ben asked:

"What did Thelma say in her last letter? Didn't she mention something about the civil rights demonstrations?"

"Yes. She wrote that the tension between whites and blacks had got worse since the shooting of J.F.Kennedy because it seemed clear that the government intended to give full civil rights to the blacks but after the Civil Rights Bill was approved there were all kinds of delaying tactics adopted by whites against integration in schools and then when Martin Luther King was shot in Memphis, the black militants said that peaceful protests would achieve nothing and began urging violent revolution. So white attitudes had hardened. She just mentioned that she and Tom had been invited by some of her former school colleagues to join a peaceful demonstration in Baltimore. That was all." Ben remarked:

"I liked Thelma very much and I am especially sorry for her that she should suffer the loss of Tom in this way. You know, Grace, we talked a few times about why we had decided to come to work in Ghana; we had that in common, she because of Afua and me because of my grandfather from Berekum. We both felt that our roots in Ghana made us want to come back here, at least for a time. Do our ancestors really influence our lives?"

"Of course they do. We think of them and of what they

did and said, and that influences us, there is an unseen tie that binds us to them."

"I suppose you could say that it all started for Thelma when her great-grandmother was captured by the Ashantis and shipped as a slave to America: a great event like slavery or a war starts off a chain-reaction in a person's life so that afterwards you may make free decisions for youself but the decisions are possible only within the framework of the great event which is working itself out and over which you have no control at all. I mean, like if you are swimming in the sea and the tide is pulling you further away from the coast, you can decide to go on swimming or just float, but you can't reach safety. In this case, a great event like slavery started a great avalanche of evil and misery, a civil war in America in which thousands of lives were lost, and even when the slaves were declared to be free they were still despised and refused their full civil rights. It takes a long time in human history before a great event like slavery comes to an end; in this situation Tom loses his life."

"You are right, Ben, but it doesn't mean that we have to be fatalistic, that we have to stop trying to repair the damage of slavery, of racial discrimination, of racism, of apartheid and skin-colour prejudice. Tom and Thelma devoted their lives to that belief and now Tom has lost his, but I feel sure that Thelma will come back to Ghana."

Then, quite suddenly, Kwesi and Amy arrived, accompanied by some of the elders and members of staff to share their sadness and Amy announced:

"The chief and elders feel bereft by Dr. McKenzie's sudden death, it is a geat blow to them. The chief has ordered a special memorial service for him, the details will be arranged when we have heard directly from his widow. May I say that for me personally I shall miss him like a brother; he was the only white man I have ever known who sympathised with and understood our Akan ways of thinking and feeling so fully".

The next days were sad ones for all those who had known Dr.McKenzie, so many had warm personal memories of his dedication as Education Officer, of his encouragement to the staff of the schools but above all of his understanding and his friendship. Everyone knew that he had had the welfare of the community at heart. Two airmail letters arrived from Thelma: the first one was to Amy:

Dear Amy, (she wrote),

When Nana, your late husband, passed away, I felt so sorry for you because you loved him and felt his loss so keenly, but at the same time I thought how brave you were to decide to go on working for the Council. Now I am trying to be brave like you; I am coming back soon to continue my work at the school and at the clinic. I feel that, in some way, I shall then be doing something to further what my husband wanted.

Will you be so kind as to pass on my request to the chief and the elders for permission to bury the ashes of my husband in the grounds of the High School and if a Memorial Service may take place there?

With warmest greetings and kindest regards,
Thelma McKenzie.

The second letter was to the Headmaster:

Dear Mr Akuffo,

You will know that I have suffered a tragic bereavement by the loss of my beloved husband whom you knew well. You can imagine my sorrow but I wish you to know that your friendship and that of all my colleagues at the school have helped me to sustain the blow and to keep up my courage. You all held him in high regard and this has comforted and strengthened me.

I shall be returning to Ghana to resume my duties at the beginning of next term; I shall travel on the Friday Pan Am plane scheduled to land at 1900 hours and I should be very grateful to be met at the airport.

> *With warmest greetings to all.*
> *Yours sincerely,*
> *Thelma McKenzie.*

Amy replied to say that the Council had chosen the Thursday in the week following her arrival for the Memorial Service at the High School and that all appropriate arrangements were being made and that she would meet her at the airport.

The Thursday, Asase Yaa day, was misty at first but about ten o'clock the power of the sun cleared the mist away. The grass in the compound had been cut short and at one side an open space had been prepared in which a small shallow grave had been dug. The singing band from the Presbyterian Church would lead the singing and four drummers from the ahemfie had rehearsed their part in the ceremony. The service had been scheduled to begin at three and long before that time crowds of mourners had been arriving, Nana and his retinue had been led to their allotted place and shortly afterwards the minister with Thelma took their places by a small table near the grave. The service began with the singing of the first verse of the well-known English hymn:

"Lead, kindly Light amid the encircling gloom, lead Thou me on.

The night is dark and I am far from home, lead Thou me on".

Then the minister prayed and they all recited the Lord's Prayer together after which he spoke about Tom.

"Nana, Elders, ladies and gentlemen, we are assembled here today to pay tribute to Dr. Thomas McKenzie, Ankobeahene, who lived and worked among us. He was born in Scotland but soon after he finished his studies at the university he came to teach in Ghana. Later he occupied a high position as an Education Officer in Kumasi and afterwards with us here in Bechemantia where he earned the respect of all of us. He was not a member of the church but he was brought up as a Christian and I personally regarded him as a shining example of the christian life, so much so that I take as my text the words of Jesus: 'Greater love has no man than this, that a man lays down his life for his friends.' He was taking part in a peaceful demonstration in America in support of full civil rights for black people when a shot was fired and in the ensuing panic Dr. McKenzie saved the life of a young black girl but in doing so lost his own life.

"You all know how he worked to establish the Brong Ahafo High School here in our town and how, as one of the Council Elders he devoted himself to our welfare. What he showed us in his life was his love for his fellow-man, he lived and died in helping others; he identified himself with us and today we honour him as one of us, and with his widow, who has returned to us to resume her work here, we mourn his passing. As part of our tribute to him we shall say together the *Nhyira* which Jesus taught us and when you do so I want you to give thanks to God for the life and work of Tom

McKenzie. (The Nhyira are from Jesus' Sermon on the Mount).

The silence was absolute, broken only by the minister's voice and the peoples' response to each phrase. He paused for the last two blessings so as to emphasise them:

Nhyira ne patafo; Na won na wobefre won Nyankopon mma.
(Blessed are the peacemakers; for they shall be named children of God).
Nhyira ne won a trenee nti wotaa won; na won na osoro ahenni no ye won dea.
(Blessed are those who are persecuted for doing right; for theirs is the kingdom of heaven).

Then Thelma and the minister took a few paces to the graveside where she laid a vase containing the ashes of her husband into the earth while the minister recited the form of words of the committal: "We commit the body of our beloved Tom McKenzie to the earth; ashes to ashes, dust to dust, in sure and certain hope of eternal life."

At a given signal the drummers broke the deep silence with the funeral stanza to Asase Yaa:

Oh spirit of the Earth,you grieve, Oh spirit of the Earth,
you suffer,
Oh Earth and the dust within you,
As long as I am dead I will be at your mercy,
Oh Earth, as long as I live I will put my trust in you,
Oh Earth which will receive my body,
We appeal to you and you will understand,
We appeal to you and you will understand.

As the last drum beat faded a new dirge was heard, the singing band and choir were chanting:

Barima 'Broni Kwabena McKenzie,
Ankobeahene, ofiri Aburokyiri, Thelma kunu barima,

Wosre wo ade a, ode rema wo.
Nante yiye! Nante yiye!
(Valiant white man Kwabena McKenzie, Ankobea chief,
who comes from Europe, the gallant husband of Thelma.
If you ask him for anything, he gives it to you!
Farewell! Farewell!)

And then, as Thelma and the minister returned to their places, the singers expressed their sympathy with the widow with the burial song:

Afua nana a ofiri Fante Morree, Akosua Morrow oo!
Ena ama-ni-ama-ba;
Na ose: owuo yi afa me ase na masiesie me ho.
Damirifua! Damirifua! Damirifua!

(Grandchild of Afua who came from Fante Morree,
Akosua Morrow, Oh!
She who gives to both woman and child!
She says: This death has taken me by surprise,
I had no time to prepare myself.
Condolences! Condolences! Condolences!)

Then the singers filed past her and one by one shook her hand in sympathy and the pent-up tears rolled down Thelma's cheeks.

The minister pronounced a benediction and the mourners made their silent way to their homes in pensive mood, their hearts filled with feelings beyond expression in words and their minds full of thoughts that lay too deep for tears. They had taken final leave of a white man who had become one of themselves and whose soul was even now on its way to the other world where the ancestors were. They had commended him both to his God and to their God; were they not the same? God was loving, compassionate and forgiving; He loved the world that He had created. Was not that enough? They felt that by this funeral they had mourned for Tom McKenzie aright and that they had truly consoled his widow. Mother Earth had received his body while the ancestors in the other world would surely welcome him with open arms and drums and horns and songs would sound for him there on the other side.

Epilogue

The last lick of paint had been given to the house near the village of Kyekyewere; Thelma had named it Comfort Cottage, and the three women, Adjowa, formerly queen-mother and the late Nana's sister, Amy, the late Nana's widow, and Thelma, Tom's widow were sitting together on the terrace looking over the dark-green forested hills below them. The village occupied an open space; its mixture of thatched and iron-sheet roofs could be seen and you could trace the terra-cotta line of the laterite road as it wound its way there. The three of them had become close friends: they shared memories of Nana and Tom and finally they had decided to live together. When you passed by the house you might see them working in the garden: they had planted a grass lawn surrounded by flowering shrubs and fruit trees and if you looked closely, you would see in one corner a hoe leaning against a pawpaw tree. It had belonged to Tom, his favourite garden tool. If you looked closer still there was a vase of flowers standing in front of a small memorial stone which bore the words, In Memory of Two Friends: Nana Oduro Panyin II and Dr.Thomas McKenzie.

Always when villagers pass by they call out a greeting and if the women are working in the garden they say *Ayekoo*! It's the traditional word of praise and encouragement given to those doing hard physical work and the workers reply: *Yeaye* (We have achieved something). Sometimes, as a joke, one of the women would look up from the weeding and utter the Twi saying: *Aboafo ye na!* (Helpers are scarce!). They would all laugh together and sometimes someone would step over the fence and take up the cutlass for a short while and as they left the women would thank them: *Dodow ye ade!* (Many hands make light work!), and wish them well. Often, Alastair and his father-in-law, occasionally accompanied by Akua and Abenaa, call on them. Together with a group of young men they have organised a transport business for cocoa and supplies to and from Sunyani and Kumasi on a co-operative system. Abenaa's father works part-time as bursar at the High School. Grace and Ben have gone to live in Bekwai, where she has become the Headmistress of a secondary school and he is a member of staff.

And the High School? It has prospered under Kwesi's leadership and its good reputation has spread; numbers have grown and there are already new buildings and new members of staff.

Finally in the Register of Births at the Council Office it is recorded that on the last Friday of April, 1971, a female child was brought into the world by Thelma Morrow McKenzie and was, of course, named Afua Thomasina. At the outdooring, you could see that she had her mother's face but her hair, her eyes and her smile came from her father. It was a day of great rejoicing!

End

Historical Notes

Chapter 1
The Battle of Asamankow 1824
The battle was really fought at Bonsaso, on the river Bonsa,which runs into the Ankobra. It was the first time that a British force had faced the redoubtable Ashanti army.

In England H.M.Consul Joseph Dupuis met Sir Charles McCarthy, who had been Governor of Sierra Leone and who was now appointed in the King's name to take control of the British forts: Cape Coast, Anomabu, James Fort (Accra), Apollonia, Dixcove, Kommenda and Winneba as well as the trading stations at Sekondi and Prampram. McCarthy took up his post in March, 1822 but many of the officers of the African Company refused to serve under him. He was helped by a few white soldiers and by a number of Fanti chiefs and Asafo companies. He made no effort to contact the Asantehene and accepted the view that there could be no peace on the coast until the power of Ashanti was broken. Before the battle he had unwisely divided his militia force into two and he faced the entire Ashanti army with only 500 men who, owing to a failure in supplies, had only twenty bullets each!

The Fanti Asafo Companies
Each town on the Fanti coast possesses its own groups of able-bodied young men organised on military lines for defence purposes. Each unit has its own flag with a special design of human and animal figures, emblems and symbols characterising the special spirit of the section. In the top left-

hand corner of the flag is a small British (since 1957 Ghanaian) flag. The flag-bearer occupies an important position: whenever the unit appears in public he leads the way, waving the large banner aloft in intricate sweeps and folds as he himself dances and whirls his body around. He is protected by a few soldiers bearing flint-lock rifles. All the units have an obosom priest and their own special headquarters or *posuban* decorated with signs and symbols and containing a shrine. Members are recruited on a paternal basis and the companies also have social duties to perform in the town.

The Slave Trade

The establishment of European colonies in the West Indies and in America gave rise to a huge demand for cheap labour on the cotton, sugar, coffee and tobacco plantations. The nearest source of supply was the west coast of Africa which became the slave market. Portugal was the first supplier, then the Dutch and the English, followed by other nations who built forts as trading stations all along the coast. Ships sailed from Europe with cargoes of European manufactured goods to West African ports, bartered these goods for human beings, for gold and ivory, sold the slaves in the West Indies or in America and returned to Europe with holds loaded with tropical crops. This so-called 'triangular trade' was immensely profitable and it has been estimated that from the middle of the 18th century when the trade was at its height, between 60 and 70 thousand slaves were shipped annually. It was only in 1833, however, that existing slaves on plantations in British territories were emancipated. In America slavery continued until the end of the Civil War in

1865. Even then, up to the end of the century, thousands of slaves were still passing through the markets of Zanzibar in East Africa.

The Address of President Abraham Lincoln at Gettysburg, 1863.

The terrible battle at Gettysburg in the American Civil War caused the deaths of 51,000 soldiers: on the Confederate side 28,000 and the Union side 23,000. In November of that year a portion of the battlefield was dedicated as a final resting-place for the men of both armies who died there. Lincoln's address lasted two minutes; his words are now immortal. Nine days after the capitulation of the southern states in 1865 Lincoln was shot dead by a fanatic southerner. This is the text of his Address.

"Fourscore and seven years ago our fathers brought forth on this continent a new nation conceived in liberty and dedicated to the proposition that all men are created equal. Now we are engaged in a great civil war, testing whether that nation, or any nation so conceived and dedicated, can long endure.

"We are met on a great battlefield of that war; we have come to dedicate a portion of that field as a final resting-place for those who here gave their lives that that nation might live. It is altogether fitting and proper that we should do this. But, in a larger sense, we cannot dedicate, we cannot consecrate, we cannot hallow this ground. The brave men, living and dead who struggled here have consecrated it far above our poor power to add or detract.

"The world will little note nor long remember what we say here, but it can never forget what they did here. It is for us, the living, rather to be dedicated here to the unfinished work which they who fought here have thus far so nobly advanced.

"It is rather for us to be here dedicated to the great task remaining before us- that from these honoured dead we take increased devotion to that cause for which they gave the last full measure of devotion; that we here highly resolve that these dead shall not have died in vain, that this nation, under God, shall have a new birth of freedom, and that government of the people, by the people, for the people, shall not perish from the earth."

The State of Pennsylvania

Charles the Second, King of England, had borrowed 16,000 pounds from his friend, an admiral of the British navy. The admiral's son, William Penn, had become a member of the Christian Quaker sect (Society of Friends) and when, after the death of his father, he requested the repayment of the loan, instead of cash he was given a grant of land in America, 300 miles long and 60 miles wide! Penn decided to found a state as a refuge for persecuted minority Christian groups in Europe like the Quakers and the Mennonites where they could live in feedom to express their Christian belief in a simple way and live according to Jesus' teaching in the Sermon on the Mount. The name means 'Penn's Forest Land' while the main town was called Philadelphia, 'Brotherly Love'. A basic principle of the constitution is complete religious toleration, there was no slavery and skin colour played no part; what mattered was living in harmony with your neighbour. The native Indians were treated with respect and lived together with the immigrants.

"Carpet-baggers and Do-Gooders"

At the end of the Civil War in America when the southern states lay in ruins, seekers after government jobs, salesmen and business men from the north arrived with their carpet bags. In the days before suitcases the large carpet bag was a useful hold-all for travellers. But these men were not all genuine; many could be compared to locusts. The southern states were devastated by war, civil administration had broken down, the plantation system was declared illegal, freed slaves had no jobs and in this situation some of these carpet-baggers from the north sought to exploit the circumstances for their own profit even when they claimed to be helping. The word 'do-gooder' is often used in this disparaging sense; they are helping to some extent but their real motive is to benefit themselves.

Ananse Stories

Kweku Ananse, the Spider Man, is the central figure of all the Akan folk-tales told to the children. Ananse is intelligent, clever, and full of ideas to benefit himself and his family but he often makes the great mistake of overreaching himself by being too greedy, too ambitious and too smart, so that he fails to achieve his aim and brings himself into real trouble. He then has to use all his ingenuity to get out of his difficulties and return to safety. All these Ananse Stories have a moral for children: not to be too selfish, think of the needs and welfare of others and not to try to be too smart and cunning so as to outwit other people.

Chapter 2
The Protectorate

In 1828 the British Government wished to leave the Gold Coast but both the traders and the coastal peoples requested London to continue; the request was granted and a grant of money was made annually to pay for the administration of the forts to the Committee of Merchants whose president, Captain George Maclean, became Governor in Cape Coast. He was one of the most able men ever to serve in that capacity: he had a revenue of only 4000 pounds a year and a police force of a mere 120 men yet his personality and his influence were such that his reputation spread widely. Chiefs from all parts brought their disputes to him; he made peace with the Asantehene, established peace along the coast and improved the economic position of the land. In a period of ten years he more than trebled the country's trade, exports (especially palm oil) increased from 90,000 to 325,000 pounds. He introduced English law alongside Akan customary law so successfully that an extra-legal jurisdiction sprang up. In 1843 the Parliament in London resumed direct responsibility for British affairs on the Coast; in 1844 a Bond was signed by the Governor and eight Fanti chiefs establishing British jurisdiction but not territorial suzerainty. In 1850, the Danes sold all their forts to the British for 10,000 pounds and as a result their vague 'protectorate' over Akuapim, Krobo and parts of Akim passed to Britain. The Governor moved from Cape Coast to Christiansborg and administered the entire coast from Keta to Beyin and inland as far as the Ashanti border. The Dutch still held their forts, the most important being Elmina.

Kroomen

In the days before modern deep-water harbours it was not easy to get ashore along the West African coast; you could only do so by being lowered from the ship into a canoe bobbing up and down alongside, then being carried swiftly by the huge waves as they approached the shore and broke into foam. To board a ship was even more difficult; in this case the canoers had to steer a way against the breakers. The local fishermen were expert but the landing of many passengers but often heavy packages and goods were left to the Kroomen. They came from Liberia; they were stocky, strong and skilful in negotiating the surf and in the important ports there grew up groups of Kroomen who earned a living by ferrying passengers and goods to and from the ships.

The Ashanti War of 1873-4

In June 1869 Ashanti forces attacked Akim and Akwamu, and crossed the Volta River into Peki. At the Basel Mission station at Anum they captured the missionaries F.A.Ramseyer and J. Kühne, and a French trader, M.G. Bonnat, at Ho. The Ashanti general, Adu Bofo, sent them, together with Mrs Ramseyer and baby son, to Kumasi and after an arduous journey through Ashanti lasting several months the captives were housed in a village near Kumasi for a time before being brought to the capital where they were treated tolerably well during their detention which lasted four and a half years. A letter was got through to them in February 1870 and on the instructions of the Asantehene they wrote their reply to the 'King of Europe' through the Dutch Governor at Elmina. This was the first direct news of the prisoners in Basel. They were still alive and being reasonably treated but the Ramseyers' baby had died on the way to Kumasi. In the same year, a second Ashanti army marched to Elmina in answer to a request from the Elmina people for help against their Fanti rivals. In 1867 an agreement between Holland and Britain to exchange forts led to widespread tribal warfare along the coast from Cape Coast to Beyin and two years later the Dutch ceded all their forts to Britain free of charge, the British paying 3,790 pounds for the stores. The Asantehene refused to recognise the transfer of Elmina Fort because he possessed the Note for Elmina by which the Dutch had agreed to pay rent for the land on which the Fort stood. Elmina was the only port on the coast through which Ashanti could trade directly with Europeans. Once again an Ashanti army marched towards Cape Coast and won victories over the Fantis at Dunkwa and Jukwa only ten miles from Cape Coast.

All-out war was inevitable and in September, 1873, Major-General Sir Garnet Wolseley was given full power to deal with the situation. From the name Sir Garnet, Akan people gave the title 'Sagrenti' to the war.

Disciple of Rousseau

The Frenchman, Jean-Jacques Rousseau (1712-1778), writer and philosopher, had a great influence in Europe during the period leading up to the French Revolution in 1789. It was a time when all institutions and traditions were under review and his writings were effective in two main ways. He asserted that at birth all human beings were equal, all were naturally good, and that all should be reared in harmony with nature so as to develop their natural aptitudes in an unforced way. He wrote a novel in 1762 called *Emil* in which he describes the proper education of the young boy, a book which changed ideas about the education of young children. Pestalozzi in Switzerland was one of his followers.

After P.E.Isert made his journey along the Akwapim Ridge in 1786, his book, *Travels in Guinea*, was a bestseller in Europe. In the book he describes how the Africans he met were living in harmony with nature and he emphasised the dignity, humanity and grace of their lives in contrast to the Africans on the coast who had been influenced for the worse by contact with traders and the slave trade. His book did much to call attention to the need in West Africa for missions and schools and to abolish the slave trade.

The second proposition of Rousseau, expressed in his book called *The Social Contract,* starts from the natural freedom and equality of all human beings. Therefore, whenever a group of people organise themselves into a state, it must be on the basis of the mutual agreement of all its citizens; the people, not the king, are sovereign. This agreement should be written in a constitution which would guarantee full civil rights to every citizen. In this way, Rousseau prepared the way for the French Revolution and for the development of parliamentary democracy in Europe.

The Moravians
The Protestant Pietistic Church called the Moravian Brethren had its main centre in Herrnhut in Saxony, Germany, from which in 1767 five missionaries were sent to Christiansborg where they were welcomed by the Danish Governor. Three of them died of malaria within three months. A further group of four was sent three years later but again fever struck and all died.

Chapter 3
Natal Day Names in Ghana

All Akans automatically bear the name of the day of the week on which they were born, and in addition, at the naming ceremony, they are given other names, perhaps commemorating an ancestor, or indicating a special family relationship, or by a number indicating the sequence among the children, Baako (one), Anan (four). A twin is designated Atta, and a baby bearing a resemblance to a deceased ancestor may be called 'Ababio' ('he has returned').

		Male	**Female**
Monday	*Dwoda*	Kwadjo	Adjowa
Tuesday	*Benada*	Kwabena	Abenaa
Wednesday	*Wukuda*	Kweku	Akua
Thursday	*Yawda*	Yaw	Yaa
Friday	*Fida*	Kofi	Afua
Saturday	*Memeneda*	Kwame	Ama
Sunday	*Kwasida*	Kwesi	Akosua

Clan Names in Scotland

Campbell and Macdonald are names of clans and children automatically bear the name of the clan of their father. There are about 200 clans each with their own distinctive tartan striped pattern when the traditional national dress is worn. Campbells and Macdonalds are two of the largest clans.

Chapter 4
Hispanics
This is the name used in the USA to denote the Spanish-speaking immigrant communities whether from Spain or from former Spanish colonial lands.

E pluribus unum
A Latin phrase meaning: ' a single unit out of many'. It is used to describe the composition of the people of the United States; so many immigrants from so many different nations joined to make one nation.

Peace Corps (USA) and Voluntary Service Overseas (British)
Since the end of the second World War these organisations have recruited young men and women volunteers, mainly trained teachers and social workers, to serve in developing and newly-independent countries.They are entirely at the disposal of the governments of the countries to which they are sent and most often work with nationals in new projects.

M.I.T.
The abbreviated form of the prestigious Massachusetts Institute of Technology in Cambridge across the Charles River from Boston,USA.

The Twi-Fanti-Ashanti Language and its proverbs
The Twi-Fanti language is the mother tongue of half the population of Ghana and is widely understood by the other half. There are three written and spoken forms, Ashanti, Fanti and Akuapem. From the beginning the Basel Mission sought to use Twi and Christaller's monumental grammar

and dictionary which represent the greatest achievement of any linguist in West Africa. It was first published in 1875. M.Cannell, an English Methodist missionary, published a grammar of Fanti in 1886 and much later, after the second World War, a third written form was introduced for Ashanti.

One of the most interesting and valuable characteristics of the language is the fact that it contains a large number of proverbial sayings; Christaller recorded 3600 in his book in 1879, while in 1951, C.A. Akrofi published 1018 of them with English translations and comments. The proverbs are the oldest source of information on the outlook on life of the Akan, their religious beliefs, as well as their traditional customs and morality. The Dictionary and the Proverbs together are a veritable encyclopedia of Akan life still authoritative today.

Parkinson's Disease

This disease was first described by the English doctor J.Parkinson (1755-1824). It is a kind of paralysis characterised by a rigidity of the body's muscular system together with trembling of the hands and limbs. It is not fatal but there is no known cure. The symptoms can be alleviated by massage and medicaments.

Chapter 6
Wolfgang Amadeus Mozart (1756-91)

This Austrian classical musician and composer was outstanding in every respect; as a child of six he was already renowned as a pianist and violinist and gave public concerts in his home town Salzburg as well as in Vienna. Before he was ten he had performed in south Germany, Paris and London. Eight inspiring symphonies were written between December 1771 and August 1772 when he was not yet 16! Everything he composed is unique and unsurpassed; he could express every human emotion from purest joy to the deepest sorrow in sublime melodious form. In addition to being a master of orchestral pieces, no one before Mozart had discovered the deep poetic richness and melancholic, plaintive tone-colour of the solo clarinet, no one before him had shown such artistry in developing solo piano melodies. Yet he died in poverty at the age of 35 and was buried in a pauper's grave!

"To swear the forbidden word"

Every Akan community possesses a 'forbidden word' which can only be spoken under certain circumstances. Often this word or name refers to calamities in the past life of the community like defeats in battle. No one mentions these events lest it could cause a repetition of the disaster or displease the ancestors. If however, someone swears and uses the forbidden word or name (*meka ntam kese*), it means that the matter is serious enough to involve the highest authority. For example, if a tribal taboo or if a community law has been violated, or if a personal dispute is of such gravity that it must come to law. 'Swearing the oath' was thus the means of bringing a case to court. The European missionaries seemed to have totally misunderstood this process and to have associated the oath as taking God's name in vain.

Chapter 7
The Congo Situation 1960-1964

On the 30th June 1960 the former Belgian Congo became an independent state with Patrice Lumumba as Prime Minister and Joseph Kasavubu as President. A few days later, the Congolese soldiers mutinied against their white officers and went on the rampage country-wide killing white and black civilians; many Roman Catholic nuns were raped, law and order broke down as tribal conflicts broke out and many Congolese suffered death. Finally, Belgium sent troops to restore order and to protect the whites still in the country, but it was only in Katanga Province in the east that relative calm was achieved and there, on the 12th July, Moise Tshombe, the son of a wealthy Katangese merchant, declared the secession of the province and took control of it from Elisabethville.

Dag Hammarskjöld, the United Nations Secretary General, was appealed to by Lumumba and the Security Council duly authorised a UN force to restore order in the Congo and to force Katanga to return to the fold. Within weeks, military contingents from 16 different countries numbering eventually 20,000 men, were dispersed throughout the Congo but were not placed under the command of the Prime Minister. Meanwhile, on the 5th September, President Kasavubu announced that he had dismissed Prime Minister Lumumba and in return Lumumba sacked Kasavubu. Into this vacuum stepped a Congolese army sergeant-major, Joseph-Desire Mobotu who seized power and set up a government of university graduates. For a time, Lumumba stayed in the Prime Minister's residence in Leopoldville, guarded on the inside by Ghanaian troops, but when he tried to escape to Stanleyville, his home base, where his deputy, Antoine Gizenga, had set up a government in exile, he was caught by Mobutu's soldiers and brought back to Leopoldville in chains. He was then flown to Elisabethville and a month later it was reported that he had been shot while trying to escape. In fact, he had been murdered on the order of the Interior Minister of Katanga and with the knowledge of Tshombe.

World opinion was outraged by Tshombe and the Security Council ordered the immediate withdrawal of all Belgian and foreign military personnel from Katanga. In September 1961 Dag Hammarskjöld agreed to meet Tshombe but on the way his plane crashed and the Secretary-General was killed. A cease-fire agreement was reached that lasted two years. The UN appointed an Irish diplomat, Dr.Conor Cruise O'Brien, to restore law and order and to take control of Katanga. Additional troops were sent from Ethiopia to help the existing UN forces. Indian units seized control of Elisabethville in the name of a united Congo in January 1963 and Tshombe fled into exile.

Tribal wars and rebellion broke out almost everywhere in the Congo on the news that the UN would withdraw. Pro-Lumumba rebels, called Simbas, captured Stanleyville in August 1964 and set up a People's Republic whereupon the regime in Leopoldville in desperation called Tshombe out of exile to become Prime Minister. With the help of mercenaries and Belgian paratroopers, 2000 whites in Stanleyville held hostage were rescued and other Simba-held towns were taken. Not long afterwards Tshombe was overthrown and General Mobutu took power and imposed a ruthless control which gave a relative element of stability to the long-suffering land.

The Group known as the Circle

An account of this organisation is given by Dr Kwame
Nkrumah in his *Autobiography,* Appendix B, published in
Edinburgh in 1957.

Chapter 8
Professor K.A.Busia

The words of Dr Busia in the London press are quoted by
Dr Kwame Nkrumah in his *Autobiography,* page 279.

Chapter 9
The Ankobeahene

All Akan large towns have a traditional chief (ohene) who
has been elected by the elders (*mpanyimfo*) and together they
are responsible for organising all customary matters. The
elders have their own stool and within the divisional bound-
ary they have specific duties. Major stools are connected with
divisional organisation while others were mainly established
to serve the omanhene. It varies from town to town how
many stools there are but invariably there are those of the
queenmother, the okyeame, a Krontihene, a Gyasehene, a
Nifahene, a Benkumhene, a Kyidomhene and an
Ankobeahene.

'Ankobea' means in English 'he doesn't go anywhere' and
his duties were always at court to help the Gyasehene in
organisation and to counsel the omanhene.

Chapter 10

The Akan Odwira annual festival

The Odwira is specially important in Akuapem and Akim; in Ashanti stress is placed on Akwasidae while in Cape Coast the main festival is called Fetu Afahye and in Elmina Bakatue. Among the Ga people their annual celebration is named Homowo.

Chapter 11

The Civil Rights Movement in the USA

On August 28th 1963, just a hundred years after Abraham Lincoln had abolished slavery in the USA, Rev. Dr Martin Luther King (1929-1968) a minister of the Baptist Church who had become the leader of the Civil Rights Movement in the USA, gave his famous speech (' I have a dream') from the steps of the huge Lincoln Memorial in Washington before a massed gathering of 200,000 people. What had happened after the end of the Civil War when the slaves in the southern states were officially free? The Civil Rights Act of 1875 gave them the same rights as whites but the Supreme Court ruled that the blacks were equal but 'separate' and the word 'separation' meant that everywhere in the USA there were separate schools for black children, separate suburbs in the towns and cities, separate sections in buses and trains, segregation in almost every area of public life. There were even separate regiments in the Army until the second World War. Then in 1954 the segregation in schools was successfully challenged when the Supreme Court ordered the integration of public schools but progress was so slow that blacks began mass protests, not only in the south but also in the cities of the north, protests which often ended in riots. President J.F. Kennedy (1917-1963), who had proposed further civil rights legislation for blacks was shot dead in November, 1963, in Dallas, and five years later, in April 1968, outside a Memphis motel, King was assassinated. In the following June, Robert F. Kennedy, (1925-1968) who had been Minister for Justice and was now a presidential candidate, was also shot dead. The grief, dismay and frustration felt by the black people of the USA led to renewed rioting in many cities across the country with much loss of life.

The speech of Martin Luther King in 1963 had by then become the expression of the long-held hopes of black Americans in their protracted struggle for full civic rights. This is part of his speech:

"I have a dream that one day this nation will rise up and live out the true meaning of its creed...

"I have a dream that one day on the red hills of Georgia the sons of former slaves and the sons of former slave owners will be able to sit down together at a table of brotherhood...

"I have a dream that my four children will one day live in a nation where they will not be judged by the color of their skin but by the content of their character."

A Review

It is a great pleasure to write this commentary on *It Happened In Ghana* by Noel Smith, for I knew him as a missionary colleague at the Presbyterian Training College Akropong. He was an affable person, a good preacher, teacher and scholar, so when I saw the title of his book, I wondered whether he was now writing thrillers or romantic novels or merely using historical romance as a gimmick for some serious message that he thinks might go down better through this medium than through normal discourse. If he wanted to write another history book like his work on *The Presbyterian Church of Ghana 1835 -1960*, could he not have used a similar format? Could the particular romance he was writing have happened only in Ghana and not somewhere else? Was the romance incidental to something else he wanted to bring to the attention of his readers?

He drops a hint in his Foreword, for it appears that what seemed remarkable to him during his stay in Ghana, especially at the Presbyterian Training College at Akropong where he worked and elsewhere, was the fact that "skin colour" was not a problem in that country. To get a better feel for the people and their culture, he not only learned to speak the local language, but also increased his knowledge, understanding and appreciation of African cultural values and usages by immersing himself in the available scholarly literature on the history and culture of the Akan written by notable Ghanaians and other researchers.

The idea of writing a historical romance emerged from

this. First, there was the urge to share this knowledge and experience of Ghana with his readers, including the friendly disposition and openness of the people to all and sundry regardless of race or skin colour. Second, he felt that he could, in the process, highlight the virtues of Africa evident in the Characters of his Historical Romance in order to combat the ignorance, pride and prejudice in the western hemisphere and its dire consequences of inequality evident in slavery (which he describes as a global catastrophe) and colonialism, both of which happened in Ghana and which made him feel ashamed in his reflective moments in that country.

He makes a few allusions to his "combat" theme early in the text, beginning with his Foreword:

Skin colour has nothing to do with personality. Africans have no prejudice towards palefaces (Foreword).

Afua Danso "was a slave girl being bought and sold for money, yet she was every bit as refined and cultured as any white woman" (p 9).

"Darkies" were considered to be primitive, ignorant, lazy, dirty, by no means as far advanced as whites, certainly inferior to them, only for hard labour in the fields and for menial tasks. But Afua was as good looking as any white woman; she was modest even without clothes, friendly, good-humoured and intelligent (p10).

Although the father was a native born citizen of the United States, Robert was classed as a slave (p.14).

How smug and unfeeling towards Africans the vast majority of whites could be, as though to be born with a white skin was an automatic claim to superiority; even the poor whites demonstrated this attitude (p.17)

Robert's experience with horses had made a favourable impact. The main thing, however, was that they were being accepted as equals by a white Family and being given the opportunity to integrate themselves into an American community which had no prejudice against Blacks (p.26).

Thus *It Happened in Ghana* also carries a positive message. Conceived as a literary work, it demonstrates, through a clearly defined plot and a series of episodes, which take place in different locations, that racial prejudice based on skin colour is not a pervasive and unalterable human condition. The principal characters who are both Black and White are embroiled in various encounters, notably wars, slave trade, colonialism and post-colonial reconstruction. Regardless of their skin colour and cultural differences, they make friends or fall in love secretly during these encounters. When they are forced to part company by the cessation of hostilities or whatever brought them together, they serve in various capacities in new locations outside their original places of domicile. They are accepted or integrated into existing social structures because of the warmth of their personalities and the manner in which they are able to adjust themselves to the pressures and challenges of new environments. Changes in the circumstances of the principal characters or their descendants enable them not only to restore broken relationships but also to identify themselves with the cause of freedom and justice or to reconnect in various ways with the development aspirations of Ghana where it all started.

I was naturally impressed by the way in which the author chose the characters, his treatment of the plot and the various episodes or contexts of action he creates from the historical and social facts available to him. What excited me most were the author's vivid historical accounts of the series of British-Ashanti wars, which started in 1824. They reminded me very much of the stories of Ashanti war strategies that my grandmother used to tell me when I was a child, for this was part of the lore on which Ashanti children were brought up. I am sure, however, that the author had a different didactic intention as indeed one can infer from the appendix of copious historical notes and the glossary of terms he provides, for human beings respect and get on well with one another when they know, understand or appreciate each other's culture or have at least the minimum basis for intercultural communication and understanding.

As the author's work will speak for itself far better than I can, I would like to end my comments here. Let me conclude by congratulating him for writing this exciting and informative Historical Romance, which not only stimulates imagination but also gives readers background historical and cultural information for their appraisal of his observations and comments. I am sure *It Happened in Ghana* will be enjoyed not only in Ghana but in Diasporic Africa, the northern hemisphere and many parts of the world interested in getting to know and understand contemporary Africa.

J. H. Kwabena Nketia
Emeritus Professor
Legon 2007

Glossary

abosom trees,	powerful spirits and lesser gods dwelling in rivers, large rocks or in shrines served by akomfo (priests).
abusua	the family, the clan and the kindred group in Akan society.
adae	a festival day occurring about once a month when the chief and certain elders enter the stool house to invoke the blessing of the ancestors.
adagio	an Italian word used in Music to describe a slow movement.
Agyeman	a praise name given to important chiefs. 'He saves the nation'.
ahemfi	a chief's palace.
asamanfo	the people in the world of the dead where all the ancestors are.
Awuraa	the Akan word for the mistress of a household.
barima	a word for man used normally in praise: manly, brave, chivalrous.
Benkumhene	the chief in charge of the left-wing units in time of war; in time of peace he had responsibility for certain towns and villages in the district.
brougham	the name of a four-wheeled one-horse carriage.
buggy	a light carriage, pulled by one horse, for one or two persons.
cassava	a tropical plant with starchy roots, a staple food in West Africa. Also called manioc.
cutlass	a cutting tool with a slightly curved blade used widely in West Africa for farming and for household uses.
genes	the factors which compose the basic structure of all human beings; they are inherited from parents and passed on at conception.
dono	dono drums are small and can be held under the left arm and played by a drum stick.

ena	a name for 'mother'.
Ewe	the name of one of the peoples of Ghana who live on the east of the country.
fontomfrom	'talking drums' normally beaten when carried horizontally on the head. The drummers walk behind and sound out proverbs and sayings.
fufuu	boiled yam beaten with pestle and mortar until soft then eaten with a savoury stew.
Golden Stool	In Ashanti the Golden Stool embodied the spirit of the entire people; it was at the same time the symbol of their unity, their power and their continuing life.
guts	a word in English for courage and determination.
hurricane lamp	a portable metal paraffin-oil lamp; its flame is protected from the wind by a glass cover.
kenkey	a ball, the size of a fist, of cooked maize meal.
kente	the expensive cloths woven in imported coloured silks in many standarised, intricate designs. The strips, about 9 cm. wide are sewn together to make a cover cloth which is worn like a Roman toga.
kyekyewere	a word meaning 'comfort'.
libation	the pouring out onto the earth of wine or other beverage to the ancestors or to a god or to Mother Earth in gratitude and supplication.
Mankata	the Akan version of McCarthy.
mulatto	a person who has one parent white and one parent black.
ntama	the usual word for the body-cloth, cotton or silk, worn in Ghana.
ntumpane	together with the fontomfrom, these 'talking drums' , usually in pairs, rest on the ground at an angle to the drummer.
Nyame	the supreme God, the most often-heard word for God among the Akan.

oburoni	the word for 'white person' from Europe(Aburokyiri).
odum	a Ghana forest tree, (chlorofora excelsa), up to 30 metres in height with huge buttress supports.
ohene	chief or king.
okro	a fruit used much in soups.
okyeame	an important official at court who is the spokesman in all interviews with the chief. Petitioners address the chief through him and he mediates the Chief's reply.
opanyin	'elder'; plural 'mpanyimfo', the elders in an Akan community who advise the chief.
Osagyefo	a praise name for a chief: 'warrior', 'defender'.
Otumfo	another praise name: 'powerful one'.
owura	the equivalent of Sir.
pals	comrades, close friends.
pawpaw	a tropical tree with a straight trunk which bears oval-shaped sweet, edible fruits. Sometimes written 'papaya'.
Sagrenti	the Akan version of Sir Garnet (Wolseley) commander of the British troops in the 1874 campaign.
share-croppers	tenant farmers who share in the value of the crop.
shingles	small, flat, rectangular pieces of wood used as roof tiles.
suman	charms,talismans,mascots,amulets which are personal to the owner which are believed to protect the wearer from evil, mischief , calamity or accident.
wari	a game played in West Africa with 48 pebbles or marbles on a board hollowed out into two parallel rows of 6 cups.
washout	a word for a useless and unsuccessful person; it is also used to describe a complete disaster or fiasco.
yam	an edible tuber in West Africa about the size of a forearm which is grown under prepared mounds of earth